BY JOHN P. MARQUAND

The Moto Series

YOUR TURN, MR. MOTO
THANK YOU, MR. MOTO
THINK FAST, MR. MOTO
MR. MOTO IS SO SORRY
LAST LAUGH, MR. MOTO
RIGHT YOU ARE, MR. MOTO

Selected Novels

THE LATE GEORGE APLEY
SINCERELY, WILLIS WAYDE

Thank You, Mr. Moto

Thank You, Mr. Moto

JOHN P. MARQUAND

LITTLE, BROWN AND COMPANY

BOSTON   TORONTO

REPUBLISHED JULY 1985

Library of Congress Cataloging in Publication Data

Marquand, John P. (John Phillips), 1893–1960
  Thank You, Mr. Moto.

  Originally published: 1936.
  I. Title.
PS3525.A6695T37 1985   813'.52   85-85
ISBN 0-316-54698-4

BP

*Published simultaneously in Canada
by Little, Brown & Company (Canada) Limited*

PRINTED IN THE UNITED STATES OF AMERICA

Thank You, Mr. Moto

CHAPTER I

I OFTEN like to think that the entire sequence of events of the afternoon and evening, which I am now trying to set down, tend to prove a theory to which I used to be partial. The theory is that man, even an individual among the pitifully small number of great ones that have risen above the mediocrity of the race, drifts rather helplessly on the current of circumstances. He cannot alter circumstances to suit himself. The Julius Caesars, the Ghenghis Khans, and the Hitlers are types tossed to the surface by half recognized subterranean forces of history, moving in the turmoil like rice grains in boiling water. I used to believe that no individual ever turned the stream of events from its course. At any rate I never tried that afternoon. Even if I had had a premonition that I could have altered a single detail of circumstances, I should not have exerted myself. I had learned from my years in China, that undue exertion of nearly any form leads to difficult consequences, and at any rate is undignified.

3

I finished the page I was writing and locked it with the rest of my manuscript in the drawer of my red lacquer desk, comfortably aware that I should probably never complete it, and that it made no great difference either way. The rather battered silver travelling clock on my desk, one of the few objects I had left to remind me that I had a past, indicated that the hour was a quarter past six, which meant that the afternoon had barely started in Peking. My perpetual calendar on the desk showed that the day was mid July.

I was buttoned in a blue Chinese robe of the latest sartorial style, and felt relaxed and comfortable. It annoyed me that it would not be suitable to continue in such a costume where I was going. I leaned back in my chair and raised my voice, but not loudly, being certain a servant was always in easy earshot. My voice mingled with the droning of the cicadas in the trees beyond my courtyard walls.

"Yao," I said. My number one boy pushed back the reed screen of the door quietly, and walked across the grey tiled floor with whiskey and a soda syphon, and we conversed in the telegraphic grammar of China.

"Lay out a clean white suit," I said. "I am going to a party at Mr. Montgomery's."

There was actually no need to tell him where I was going, because like any other servant in Peking,

4

Yao knew his master's social engagements as accurately as he knew his weaknesses.

"You may have dinner ready at nine o'clock," I added. "I do not know whether I will be back for it or not. I do not know whether I will bring guests back with me or not, but if I do come back I shall want a good dinner."

My vagueness did not upset him. I doubt if there is any place in the world, where one may be as non-committal and still be confident of perfect service as in Peking. I knew that my white suit and my white shoes would be immaculate, and they were. Yao helped me on with my coat and knelt down to arrange the cuffs of my trousers.

"Get me another handkerchief," I said, "and I have no money in my pocket."

"Last night," said Yao, "you used up all your money."

"Very well," I said, "lend me ten dollars."

Yao was my banker at times, and not any more dishonest than several other financiers I have dealt with. I walked through my courtyard where the yard coolie was watering a border of blue and white flowers, past the spirit screen which guarded the red door of the grey outer wall. The door was opened almost automatically by the door keeper, who I knew would be ready to perform that function at any hour of the day or night that might bring me home. My ricksha with my puller, in clean white clothes, was ready at the gate. A moment later we were out of the narrow residential alley, rolling south along a broad street toward the Legation Quarter. My boy was running smoothly and seemingly tirelessly, as a good ricksha boy should run. The sights and sounds of Peking in summer seemed to move on either side of me, unrolling as a scroll painting might unroll, changing with each street corner but never really changing. I could come near to seeing with my eyes closed, simply from the sounds I heard. A deeper note in the patter of slippered feet told me that we were passing close by the pink stucco wall of the Forbidden City, where the yellow-tiled roofs of its pavilions rose above it, shimmering silkily beneath the blue sky that was growing darker with the drooping of the sun. There was a high squeak of a water carrier's barrow, the rumble of a man-drawn cart, a patter of donkeys' hoofs, a whistling of a trained flock of pigeons in the sky, the blare of a radio from the door of an open shop and the noise of a motor horn, but such sounds did not disturb a pervading impression of serenity. I could hear the brass castanets of the sweetmeat vender and the tinkling of the fan venders' bells, and the cry of a melon seller. Those sounds all came together into an endless wave of sound, peaceful, enveloping, the noise of China where men lived and died according to fixed etiquette, where nothing mattered very much, except

6

perhaps tranquillity. I felt tranquil enough at any rate and I was very glad to be so. I was pleased with the thought that nothing would ever change the city very much and that I was a part of it in a way, as much at any rate as a foreigner might be. I took a fan from my pocket, a fan with a poem on it, about cranes and lotus blossoms, which my Manchu friend Prince Tung had given me.

There were a great many rickshas already near the willow tree by the Montgomerys' front gate. The ricksha coolies were squatting beneath the tree, discussing the eccentricities and peccadillos of their masters and their mistresses. They would be glad to wait there until two o'clock in the morning, if necessary, without complaint. A band was playing on the terrace of the Montgomery house, which was a two-story European structure, but the strange cosmopolitan life of Peking moved easily around it. Nearly everyone knew everyone else down to the last detail of scandalous gossip, and the knowledge that there was nothing hidden except by the scant mercies of convention was rather reassuring. The British, Russian, German, Italian, Japanese and the Chinese officials were there. Everyone was there. White-robed servants were passing cocktails and appetizers. Mr. Montgomery, fat and perspiring, in his white silk suit, shook hands with me.

"Glad to see you aboard, Tom," he said. There was

something buoyantly reminiscent of old days in America about Joe Montgomery, which frequently made me restless. My hostess, Elsa Montgomery, drew me aside.

"Tom," she said. "Don't you feel nervous?"

"Why?" I asked.

"Because the army has been drawn out of the city," she said. "It has been a definite fact since yesterday. There are only the police. Anything might happen." A boy passed with a tray of cocktails. I took one.

"Elsa," I said. "You know that nothing ever happens."

"But aren't you interested?" she asked.

"Not in Chinese politics," I said. "It doesn't pay to be, because they change too fast."

"You must know a great deal about them though," she said. "You play around with the Chinese so much, but you never say anything."

"Meaning you don't approve of my native friends?" I answered. "Well, there's nothing really to say. Everything goes on. I'm writing a book about that."

"Why Tom!" she said. "I didn't know you were writing a book. I didn't know you were doing anything."

"As a matter of fact," I answered, "I didn't know I was writing a book myself until a week ago. It's better to say you're doing something than nothing out here, isn't it? Otherwise one might be misunder-stood."

Then she turned away from me and said: "Why, how do you do, Mr. Moto. You know Mr. Moto, don't you Tom?"

Mr. Moto and I had met on several occasions. He was a small rather chunky Japanese, in well fitting European clothes, who appeared occasionally — perhaps three times a year — in Peking and stayed at his Consulate and disappeared without warning. Mr. Moto shook hands effusively and drew in his breath politely.

"Oh yes," he said. "Oh yes. Mr. Nelson and I are very good friends. Oh yes." His eyes which were rather protruding moved toward me searchingly. His smile was nervous and determined. "So you are writing a book!" he said. "I did not know."

I looked back at him and we both stood smiling, determinedly and heartily, seemingly waiting for the other to grow tired.

"It would be interesting if you wrote one too," I said. "Let me read yours, and you can read mine."

Mr. Moto laughed artificially. "Ha! Ha!" he said. "That would be very funny. You are such a clever man, and I am so very stupid."

Though it was true he laughed, I have a tolerable faculty for sensing moods. In Mr. Moto's manner toward me there was a new empressment. He was

9

no longer lightly casual; his narrow eyes were analyzing me as he smiled. I was aware that he was trying to place me in the order of recognized personages and I guessed the reason for his interest. It lay in the feebly jocular remark that I was writing a book.

"Your book," said Mr. Moto, "what is it about?"

"The manuscript is in the drawer of the red lacquer desk in my sitting room," I said. "Drop in any time and read it, when I am out, Mr. Moto, but I am afraid it isn't the sort of thing you're interested in."

"Thank you," said Mr. Moto and he bowed, "thank you very much. Good bye."

It seemed to me that it would be hard to find a place in the world where so many types and interests mingled in apparent friendliness, as there in the Montgomerys' garden. There were the Chinese and the Japanese and Russians, for instance, instinctively each of them suspicious of the other, but all affable and smiling; bound together temporarily by an American jazz tune, that cultural gift of our nation to every outpost of the world.

"Elsa," I said to Mrs. Montgomery. "I'll tell you something, and remember I told you, when it happens. There is going to be some new sort of political trouble here. I have found it out just now."

"Just now?" said Mrs. Montgomery. "Just now, this minute?"

"Has it ever occurred to you," I asked her, "that every time in the last year when there has been any sort of crisis or tension in North China — and believe me, there has been a lot of it — that Mr. Moto has always appeared? Not that it really matters. None of these things really matter."

"I've heard other people say that it is a Mr. Takahara who makes the trouble," she remarked. "Do you know him?"

"No," I said. "It doesn't matter, does it?"

"Nothing does matter to you, does it?"

"Elsa," I said, "when you get as old as I am —"

"You're not so old," she interrupted.

"When you get as old as I am intellectually," I said. "If you ever do. You'll find there's only one thing that matters — keeping out of trouble."

She may have been aware of some implication in what I said. At any rate she did not seem altogether happy, and I no longer interested her.

"Here comes Major Best," she said in a tone which indicated plainly enough that Major Best was more interesting. He was walking toward us, easily and competently, across the courtyard, holding a highball glass in his hand, as he had walked a hundred times before. I only know now that there was a tragic fatality in his seemingly casual appearance that afternoon. I only know now that that whole afternoon was a part of a drama where all the characters mingled, utterly unconscious of what was to happen. When I think of it in that manner, the Montgomerys' garden, with its green bushy trees against a sky that was dustless and clear, assumes the proportions of a stage. All the people there in my memory seem now to have been walking in a hard bright light . . . the Chinese in their silk robes the only persons clinging to a national costume, the rest of us in European clothes, but nearly all of us with the mark of the Orient on our faces. Some made weary by it, some sodden and some violent.

Major Jameson Best was a recognizable type, just as, I suppose, we all were. His white clothes were perfect like the clothes of most Englishmen, surrounding a body which steady exercise kept perpetually fit. The cut of his hair, growing grey at the temples, was perfect. His face had all the sharp angles and lines of a British face, those singularly determined, conventional lines, not to be changed by any experience; but somehow one knew very well that Jameson Best had seen plenty. The things he had seen were written in the corners of a tight, even mouth, and in the wrinkles around his eyes.

There was a reflection in his eyes such as occasionally appears in the eyes of a jaded traveller. Though there were mysterious suspicious gaps which no one could fill, everyone knew parts of his history. He had been to Tibet and Turkestan. He had been captured by the bandits in Manchuria. It was said he could speak a dozen dialects but he never displayed the knowledge. All of that was reflected in his eyes. They were a pale washed-out grey, level and mirthless even when he laughed.

He came toward us, walking softly.

"Well," he said to Mrs. Montgomery. "Everybody's here, what? And now Nelson's here it's perfect, what? Nelson, how about a spot of dinner with me tête-à-tête? We haven't settled the affairs of the nation for a long while, have we young fellow? You and I will cut off together when Mrs. Montgomery throws us out, eh what?"

"Thanks," I said, "I'd like to, Best."

He smiled; there was a flicker in his eyes which was not humorous. "That's topping," he said. "Join me when you're ready, eh?" He took a sip from his highball, bowed and moved away. I looked at Elsa whose increasing restlessness indicated that she wished me to move on also.

"The war was won," I said, "on the playing fields of Eton."

13

"What's got into Jamy?" said Elsa. "I didn't know you two were such friends. I thought — "

"You thought he had other interests," I remarked. "Which girl is it now?"

"The new one," said Elsa. "Don't say you haven't heard? The one who came out here last Spring and keeps staying and staying. Miss Joyce, of course. She's dancing on the terrace now." I glanced toward the terrace long enough to see that Major Best was not moving in that direction.

"I didn't know that you and Jameson Best were such friends," Elsa said again.

"Neither did I," I answered. "Don't you see what's happening?"

"No," she said, "do you?" The boy passed with a tray of cocktails and I took another, my third.

"Another affair," I said. "The Major wants to be seen leaving here with me. He wants everyone to know just how he is spending his evening. He knows that I generally go home early. Well, it doesn't matter."

She began to laugh. "Tom," she said, "that's too clever to be right."

"No," I told her, "it's too easy not to be. The human mind is almost always the same, Elsa. If you'll excuse me, I think I might dance now."

"With Miss Joyce?" she asked.

"Perhaps," I said. "It doesn't matter, does it?"

"Probably not," said Elsa, "but I am a little sorry for Miss Joyce."

"You're probably right," I told her. "But it doesn't matter, does it?"

CHAPTER II

I DRANK a fourth cocktail and moved toward the terrace. I had seen Eleanor Joyce, this girl of whom Mrs. Montgomery had spoken, often enough during the last few months. In a community as small as the foreign community of Peking everybody meets, and a stranger is always welcome. I had not suspected until that afternoon that Eleanor Joyce might be that kind of girl, as one delicately puts it. The idea interested me and a sort of mental upset occurred which had happened often enough before in the lives of casual males. Eleanor Joyce ceased to be an abstraction, and became a person. I stood on the edge of the terrace, waiting with a new interest until I saw her.

The dancers were moving on the terrace, idiotically, aimlessly, when one comes to think of it. I found myself watching them with an odd sense of embarrassment for their behavior, contrasting their movements with tribal dance rhythms. When I did this the whole affair of the dance descended to a primitive sort of plane, that had to do with biology and taboos and natural selection. The dancing was not really as good as most unsophisticated folk dancing. The slow steps and the polite turnings were stylized and vapid. As I stood there I had an impression of the whole world I knew falling into a drowsy dance, moving to an inhibited syncopation. I could imagine all the foreigners in Peking turning to that impulsive beat. Something was moving us along ridiculous lines, something that none of us recognized and that none of us understood. Behind the deepening blue of the North China sky an orchestra of the gods that made us all ridiculous was playing, enormous and timeless.

I saw the faces I knew move past me, some amused, some intense, some languid. One could not help wondering what force of circumstance had gathered these dancers together, strangers in a strange land from every end of the earth. Some had run from disillusion only to find more of it. Some had run to escape disgrace and probably had found that running did no good. Some of us had come there seeking something new and there was nothing new. But there was one thing which we all had in common — a certain dangerous initiative, not possessed by our countrymen at home. I saw the dancers moving past me, young, old, plain or beautiful. It made no difference which, for they all had a certain sameness, a common wistfulness, a common loneliness, a common sense perhaps of being together in a land where they were not particularly wanted.

The beat of the music quickened and Eleanor Joyce moved past me, lightly adjusted to the music's unexpected change. For a moment she was so close I could have touched her. For a moment she was distinct, in focus, while all the other dancers were blurred; then she was lost again. She had appeared and disappeared, as irrationally as friends and acquaintances in a lifetime; and the dance was like a miniature of human existence after I saw her, as steady, as commanding, and as meaningless. She had been dancing with young Boldini of the Italian Legation. She had been leaning away from him, laughing at something he was saying, giving a hint, probably intentional, of a nymph struggling in a satyr's arms. She had been pure and bright at that moment, probably the result of an optical illusion, but the impression was desirable and I had no great wish to analyze it. She had been dressed in green and brown, a tailored dress of chartreuse green foulard, a brown belt, brown sandals, brown trimming on her hat; and arms and legs were consciously burned to a golden brown. She might have been in any one of a hundred country clubs, or at a European watering place, instead of on the Montgomerys' terrace in the Legation Quarter of Peking. She was as finished in color and line as one of the year's newest motor models. I could imagine, as I had before when I had seen her, that she had as little individuality, should one bother to lift the hood. Yet I knew that she must be different, or she would not have been there that afternoon. She was not the first girl I had seen come to Peking, out of nowhere, to stay a while and disappear. She was not an adventuress. I wondered what she wanted. I wondered what the place gave her, what she saw, what she thought — probably almost nothing. Then I saw her again and I stepped toward her across the terrace.

"Please," I said to Boldini and then I was a part of the dance. I was holding her in my arms, quite impersonally, in a close conventional embrace. She smiled at me quickly — even teeth, firm chin, brown eyes that sparkled as she smiled, dark brown hair.

"Hello," she said, "I haven't seen you for a long while."

"I don't go out much," I said.

"No," she said, "I know you don't." She glanced at me sidewise. "You're rather eccentric, aren't you?"

"Perhaps," I said. "Everyone gets eccentric who stays out here for a while. I am tired of dancing. Are you?"

"But you've just started dancing," she said. "You can't be tired."

"I mean I'd like to talk to you," I said.

"I've often wondered if you ever would," she answered. "You've had chances enough. I wonder what makes you want to now."

"Well," I said, "it doesn't matter, does it?"

"No," she said, "but I am very flattered, really. I suppose you think you're being nice, don't you?"

"No," I said, "not very. I was standing there and I began to think about you, that's all."

We sat down in two chairs beside a lotus pool a few yards away from the terrace.

"What were you thinking about me?" she asked.

"Rather impertinent things," I said. She looked hard at me through the dusk.

"I suppose you talk to everyone this way," she remarked. "I don't mind it really. Well, what were you thinking?"

"I was wondering what brought you here," I said. "If one stays here long enough one wonders that about all sorts of people. There must be something here you like because you've stayed."

She leaned back in her chair and looked up at the sky.

"I like the world," she said. "I left home to see the world."

"Have you seen it?" I asked.

"Quite a good deal," she said, "but not enough. Why shouldn't I?"

"No reason," I said. "It isn't even unusual as long as your family don't mind."

She smiled at me. "As a matter of fact, they don't approve of it," she said. "I rather thought you would. Why shouldn't I? Men see the world. You've seen it haven't you?"

"Yes," I said.

"And now you're tired of seeing it? You're trying to get away from it now. Well, I'm not tired. I never will be."

"Probably not," I told her. "If you call this seeing the world, but you'd get tired if you really saw it. As it is, you'll only get into trouble. That's what always happens to a girl who wanders about indefinitely alone."

Miss Joyce looked at me again. Her lips curled up faintly.

"Are you going to protect me, Mr. Nelson?" she asked.

"No," I said. "I wasn't thinking of that — not this afternoon."

"What were you thinking of?" she asked. I offered her a cigarette and took one myself.

"I was thinking if you really must get into trouble, Miss Joyce," I said, "that you'd do very well to get into trouble with me."

Miss Joyce tapped the end of her cigarette delicately. Her face was vague in the growing dusk but I saw that she was amused.

"That's very delicately put," she said. "I suppose you know what the answer ought to be."

"Yes," I said. "The answer is 'Thank you very much Mr. Nelson, but I am quite able to look out for myself.' That isn't the real answer, of course. It's just as well it isn't."

"You're not being very polite?" she asked.

"No," I said, "I don't suppose I am, but it doesn't matter, does it?"

"Then you might as well go on," she said. "Why do you think I might refuse?"

There seemed just then no harm in being frank and perhaps I felt that it might do her good. There was something about her poise and complete assurance that made me wish to puncture it.

"You're too careful, I suppose," I said. "You have an instinct for self-preservation which will keep you on nice boats and with nice people until you find a vice-president of a reputable trust company to marry. In the meanwhile, you can see the world, a somewhat antiseptic world where there will be no malaria or tropical diseases, where there will be personally conducted tours to interesting places and where the latest style of dress is always available. By the way, that's a most successful dress you're wearing now, Miss Joyce."

22

She dropped her cigarette on the grass and stepped on it. "Do you really think I'm like that?" she asked.

"Yes," I said, "rather, but it doesn't matter, does it?"

"I wish," she said and her voice was sharper, "that you wouldn't use that phrase again."

"Very well," I said. "Why not?"

"Because it's too much like you, Mr. Nelson," she said. "I should rather be like the person you think I am than like the person I think you are."

"Go ahead," I answered. "It's only fair to give me your opinion. What sort of a person do you think I am?"

"Rather undesirable," she said. "An American gone native. I've seen them in Paris and I've seen them here. We can't stand change of environment. Now an Englishman keeps his own world about him."

"Oh quite," I said. "Jolly well so, like Major Best. The war was won on the playing fields of Eton."

"Yes," she said. "It was. Not by crawling into a corner on a small income and allowing oneself to be pampered by Chinese servants, and allowing everything to drift by and becoming immersed in Chinese culture."

"You know a good deal about me," I said.

"Yes," she answered. "Everyone talks about nothing except personalities here. You're finished, Mr. Nelson. Pretty soon the Chinese dogs won't growl at you any more. I've begun but I hope I won't end in the way you have."

"I'm sure you won't," I said. "The dogs will always take you for an American girl, but it doesn't matter, does it?"

I used the phrase unconsciously. I had never thought of myself as being finished until she had spoken.

"You're probably right," I added, "but I'd rather finish here than anywhere else in the world."

"Yes," she said, "it's decorative and comfortable." Then she looked up. Someone had moved in front of us and I knew the talk was over. Mr. Moto was standing bowing.

"Do you know Mr. Moto?" asked Miss Joyce.

"Oh yes," said Mr. Moto, "oh yes. Mr. Nelson and I are very good friends. He has been talking to you about his book perhaps."

"No," I answered, "not exactly. I'll never finish that book. Miss Joyce knows I won't."

Mr. Moto bowed to her. "Perhaps Miss Joyce would care to dance," he said. Miss Joyce looked at me and smiled.

"It's a way to see the world," she answered. "I should be delighted, Mr. Moto."

CHAPTER III

TIME of late years had begun to move past me easily. Day elided smoothly with night, and I had begun to accept the fact, with a subtle sort of resignation which was not unpleasant. I had been restless once. I had struggled against time. I had had desires. I had filled my days with activities which could not be encompassed by hours, but the timelessness of that city where tradition and where the past mingled indefinably with the present, where the modern phrase of politeness was an apology for disturbing one's neighbor's chariot, had made me broad-minded about time. I looked at my watch and found without surprise that the hour was getting on to half past eight. A middle-aged Chinese in a long black robe spoke to me — Prince Tung. He spoke in the bird like, bell like tones of his native tongue, every phrase perfect, every gesture a mirror of etiquette, that made my conversation with Eleanor Joyce, which was still running through my mind, seem crude and nakedly barbarous.

"You have not been lately to my poor house," he

said. "I have missed you. There are the crickets; you have not seen the crickets."

His words brought me back to the other side of my life which touched upon China. It brought me back to a world which was shifting, enigmatic, fascinating. It was a world which was dying perhaps but one which I respected. It was a brutal world, a merciless world, but one which was inconceivably cultivated and polite, with a cultivation that rose above sordidness and disrepair and above the annoyances of the present. I admired Prince Tung intensely and was proud that he honored me with a casual friendship. Prince Tung came of a Manchu family which had been powerful at court in the days of the Empire. He had seen the Forbidden City as a boy and could describe the great days vividly. Like most of the Manchus he had been improvident with money and now he gave evidence of being very poor. He was withdrawn from politics; he spent most of his time in part of his ruined palace, near the northern gate of the city, writing poetry on scrolls with his brushes, but his tastes were catholic and foreigners amused him. If his amusement was contemptuous, his manner never showed it. He had an ingrained politeness, cultivated by a slavish childhood study of the classics.

"You are amused, my master?" I said to him.

"Yes," said Prince Tung. "I am diverted. Your

people always divert me. I say this to you because you will understand, too well perhaps for your own good."

Prince Tung smiled and placed his delicate hands inside his sleeves.

"That young woman you were speaking to, for instance. I never can understand. Is she well bred?"

"Yes," I said. "Decidedly so, I think."

"Well," said Prince Tung. "That is very interesting. I never can understand."

"We were talking together frankly," I told him. "She told me I was finished."

He did not grasp my meaning at first and I had difficulty in explaining the phrase in Chinese.

"Oh," said Prince Tung. "At length I see. What is your honorable age? I have forgotten."

"Thirty-four," I said.

"Then she is very nearly right," said Prince Tung. "You should have sons by now who are grown to men. Personally I was married at fifteen and besides I have had six concubines. My family is large and I no longer worry. You should have your birds and your walks and conversations. You should no longer worry."

"I don't very much," I said.

"Very much is not adequate," said Prince Tung. "For example, I will tell you something. Things are very bad in the city to-day. A merchant, one of my best friends, has sent several boxes for safekeeping to the Legation bank this afternoon. I shall do the same to-morrow, but I am not worried."

"What things are very bad?" I asked. I knew he would not answer me when I asked him for he never liked a direct question.

"It is nothing," he said. "It has been said also that certain persons who frequently concoct trouble are about. The country is being clawed again by the barbarians. It is bitter that we are living through the period of turmoil which invariably follows the conclusion of a dynasty. These times have always been uncomfortable but they will pass."

"Are you worried about your property?" I asked.

Prince Tung smiled again. "I have never worried about my property," he said. "There is nothing I can do." His reply did not exasperate me as it might have a few years back.

"But you have friends, you have influence," I said.

"Perhaps," said Prince Tung. "Until the time arises. One can never tell."

Then I heard Major Best calling me. His voice was clipped and matter-of-fact and reassuring.

"I say, Nelson," he called. "Are you ready now?"

The last red glow of the sunset was on the street outside. The ricksha lamps were lighted. Major Best laid his hand on my arm. I felt his fingers on the sleeve of my coat, closing on my arm, more tightly than was necessary.

"I say," said Best. "Did that Prince Tung Johnny say anything to you?"

"He said things were bad in the city," I answered. "Why?"

I heard the Major draw in a deep breath and he dropped my arm.

"I saw a man in the street to-day," he said. "I can tell a Chinese face in a crowd. He saw me too. I hope he didn't know I knew him."

"Why?" I asked.

"Because my life wouldn't be worth tuppence," said Major Best. "Come. We've time for a spot of whiskey before dinner."

I looked at him, not particularly startled, for one deals in exaggerations so often that they do not mean much. I have heard plenty of people say that their lives would not be worth tuppence if they did not arrive in time at the Jones' party. I looked at Jameson Best and I could not see his face clearly. Then I remembered that Peking is probably the safest city in the world.

CHAPTER IV

OUR rickshas padded through the gate of the wall of the Legation Quarter and turned right and then left, on Hatamen Street. It was broad like all the streets of North Chinese cities. Police with revolvers in olive drab uniforms were directing the traffic. The open fronts of shops were squares of light. The Chinese characters above their doorways were dim above them, and Hatamen Street was a river of sound. The falsetto chant of Chinese voices and Chinese laughter erased the disturbing thoughts that were in my mind. Eleanor Joyce had said that I was finished, but her voice no longer bothered me, for it was lost in that sea of other voices, in that surge of humanity about us. The smell of Chinese cooking came pleasantly to my nostrils. There was a broad tolerance emanating from that conglomeration of sounds and smells that gave me a love for the city of Peking. It was a noble city with its walls and avenues, its hidden temples and its palaces. It was a city of the imagination, a city of the spirit falling into a dreamlike ruin; falling into memories as fantastic as the figures on a Chinese scroll; always changing but never changed.

There was that realization, comforting and complete, that the high grey walls of the Tartar City were guarding us; that the pavilioned towers above the gates were staring out into the night, warding off the evil spirits from an uncertain world outside. The walls were shutting out the clamor of South China, the floods and the starvation of the Yellow River and the sinister vacancy of the mountain passes that stretched northward like huge steps, beyond the ancient Great Wall to the Mongolian Plateau. Peking was designed by its builders to resist evil fortune. Even its straightest streets had occasional eccentric curves designed to break the dangers of symmetry. The courtyards of its houses were designed so that only harmonious spirits should enter and, on the whole, everything had been done well.

For many years Jameson Best had used Peking as a starting point for his travels and had kept a small house there on one of those innumerable narrow alleys, so characteristic of this city, which are bounded by high courtyard walls, each alley so like the next as to be as indistinguishable to the stranger as the features of the Chinese race. Jameson Best's house had once been a single courtyard in one of those labyrinthian palaces of the old regime, that

31

had once covered several acres of ground in a series of courts and buildings and gardens. The gates and the walls leading to further courts of that old palace had been bricked up long ago, so that Jameson Best's dwelling was securely shut off into a single unit of an entrance court with servants' quarters, ending in a low building which was a dining room and reception room. This opened in turn into a small garden surrounded by tiled roofed buildings, containing the Major's bedroom, his store room and his library. Our ricksha coolies shouted at some pedestrians who made way for us in the narrow alley. We jolted over ruts, the legacy of last week's rain.

"We'll have our drinks in the study," Major Best said. The study was a long room with carved, painted beams supported by red wooden pillars. There were bookcases along the wall, containing a good collection of Orientalia. Some animals' heads and several of the Major's rifles were above the books, and also a Chinese painting on silk of a tiger — snarling and ready to spring. On the floor were several tiger skins. The Major waved me to a wicker armchair and his servant brought in a tray with whiskey and glasses. Major Best stood and lifted his highball glass. He was smiling, but those pale grey eyes of his seemed to be staring at nothing.

"Cheerio!" he said, then turned and looked about

the room as though he expected to find something wrong. Apparently he did not.

"I've always liked this room," I said.

"Yes," he answered. "Snug, isn't it?" And he glanced carefully at the paper covered windows.

I watched him, wondering why it was I did not wholly like him and why I was never comfortable with him. I attributed this uneasiness to his eyes and to the perpetual coldness of his glance. It was his eyes that made him ugly. As he stood with his back to the snarling tiger on the wall I could understand the urge that made him hunt and travel. He had the proper quietness, just the requisite coldness and just the precise physique. I reminded myself again that he would not have asked me without a definite reason. Then in the midst of sipping my whiskey I discovered that he had entirely forgotten me. He was still standing looking at the window so intently that he started when I spoke.

"I saw Miss Joyce this afternoon," I said.

"Ah?" The Major raised his eyebrows. "Yes? But let's not mind her now."

I looked at the Major steadily. "I'm broad minded, Best," I said.

"Ah!" said the Major. "Quite! You and I have been around a bit, eh what?"

I had been around a bit, perhaps not exactly as

Best's tone suggested, but I did not tell him so. Instead I made a tactful effort to find why I was there.

"Best," I said. "You act as though you had something on your mind. Not a guilty conscience?"

His eyes met mine frankly and accurately as though he were looking at me over the barrel of one of his rifles.

"I haven't much conscience," he said. "Lost it somewhere I fancy. Don't remember when."

I laughed and set down my glass. "Major," I said, "you'll be a bad hat some day."

Major Best stepped toward me so quickly that I thought he was angry, but his intention was only to refill my glass. His voice was coldly jovial, over the swish of the soda water.

"Was a bad hat when I left the army, young fella," he said. "Some while ago, too — that."

It occurred to me that there is nothing in the world as bad as a well bred Englishman but I did not explain my thought. I only wanted to find out what he wanted. Nothing more. "Well," I said, "it doesn't matter, does it?"

Then I knew that the amenities were over. Best sat down close beside me. He looked toward the door and back at me.

"Nelson," he said. "There *is* something I want to talk about — an unpleasing sort of subject. I've marked you out. You don't mind my doing that."

"You flatter me," I said. "I wonder why you've picked on me?"

The Major rested his fingers on my arm again, strong, steely fingers. Who was he, I wondered? What had his past been? Why should we two be sitting here? I remember exactly what he said because his answer was characteristic of the place and of the life we led.

"I'll tell you why," he said. "Because of a phrase you use. 'It doesn't matter, does it?' And it don't matter, not a tinker's damn. You've never asked me what I'm doing here. Though you're the quiet sort, I rather believe you know your way about. You're respected in certain quarters, more than most men. You've got a way with the Chinese Johnnys. You understand them better than most white men. They like you because you mind your own business. You've never tried to get anything from them, either their souls or their money, and that is rare, damned rare."

"You may be right," I said. "Miss Joyce told me I'd gone native just this afternoon."

"Young fella," said Major Best, "we're talking about Chinese now. Did you ever hear," he lowered his voice to such a soft pitch that it startled me, "of a Johnny called Wu Lo Feng?"

I searched back in my memory through a gallery of names and faces, through bits of talk I had heard

35

of the chaotic whirl of China, where war lords and politicians had appeared and disappeared.

"I only recall him vaguely," I said. "He's a bandit, isn't he? He was mentioned as being connected with the communist uprisings. He headed an outfit three years ago called the Ragged Army."

Major Best nodded. "Quite," he said. "This Wu is interestin'. A nice interesting history. He got swept out of a village at the tail end of Honan when he was twelve years old, into the army, and he's been fighting ever since. The Chinese army is a toughening experience — if you live to be successful. You know his kind. One of his tricks is to blow his prisoners up."

I lighted a cigarette. "He wouldn't waste powder for that," I said obtusely. The Major set me right at once.

"Not powder," said Best softly. "Not powder. He simply sets a straw beneath his subject's epidermis. Then everybody interested takes a blow on the straw and the prisoner blows up — quite like a balloon. You've heard tell of it? I didn't believe it possible but it is. It's very painful — and not uninteresting. I saw Wu do it myself in the mountains outside of Kalgan. The subject, Nelson, blows up like a balloon and then he bursts — my word for it. Wu blew up one of my donkey boys. Very interesting."

"Yes?" I said. "Since you're here I take it they didn't operate on you, Major."

"No," he said. "It was only an exhibition put on for my benefit for purposes of ransom. One gets used to that sort of thing, given time to live. But this Wu is able. Away above the average, without much of the racial indirectness. Chatty — nice and chatty — but devilishly logical. I'd put him above the old Marshal of Manchuria for brains, which is in the nature of a compliment. Have another spot?"

"Thanks," I said. "Tell me some more about Wu." I knew that he was leading up to something. Major Best smiled and his voice made me understand that he respected Wu.

"He's a Johnny who knows what he wants," the Major said, "and where his bread is buttered. I know — because Wu and I did a little business once."

"What sort of business?" I asked.

"Curio business," said Major Best, "in a tomb. But that doesn't matter, does it? Wu, he's game for anything — provided it means money. And now, right now, this Wu is in Peking." There was a forced levity in the Major's voice, but his casual words concealed something which was unmistakably ugly.

"So he's the one you saw?" I asked.

Major Best moved and the wicker in his chair

creaked. "Righto," he said. "I won't forget Wu's free. Oh no! I saw him in Brass Street this afternoon, in blue coolie clothes. He looked up as I went by. Thin, high North China face, flat nose and a little amusin' mouth. The sort you might call a rosebud mouth, if he was white. A kissable mouth on a face like paste, not prepossessin'. Wouldn't like it if he thought I knew him. We know too much about each other to be exactly friends."

"What's he doing here?" I asked. The other's earnestness had made me interested.

"Young fella," said Major Best, "I don't know, but I don't like his being here, and if you knew me better you'd know that I'm broad minded, as a rule. I'll know what he's doing to-morrow. I've got ways of knowing."

"Have you?" I asked.

"Laddy," said Major Best. "Don't ask questions. If he's doing what I think he is, there's where you come in."

"Suppose I don't want to come in," I suggested.

Major Best smiled. "You won't come in far," he answered. "All I ask of you is this. Come here to see me at nine o'clock to-morrow morning. If he's doing what I think he is, I want you to take me to Prince Tung. It might be that your friend the Prince and I could do a little business."

Major Best was watching me with those unflickering eyes, so accurately, so intently, that I knew he was deadly serious, even if I were not able to understand the cause. Nevertheless, he had laid a number of cards frankly on the table, rather skillfully too, and I gave him credit for that. I looked at the Major; his eyes were still on me; his face was still set in those rugged conventional lines. He had confessed that he was no better than he should be, not a damaging or astonishing confession perhaps. He had tacitly confessed that he was a grave robber and he had been on the verge of confessing something else. He had spoken of means of gaining information and then he had checked himself. I looked about his room again; it was comfortable, almost luxuriously comfortable for the room of a cashiered British army officer, and I knew that Best had been cashiered because he had as good as told me so. It had seemed none of my business until then, but now I wondered how the Major made his money. He and Mr. Wu made a pretty pair; they were perfect examples of my theory that men appeared from circumstance. They were perfect patterns of characters that might be expected to rise out of the turmoil of the East, both clever, as the Major had said. Each knowing exactly what he wanted.

"Best," I said, "I came out here to be quiet. I came out here because I didn't do so well at home, but not because I had to. I quarrelled with a number of people, but I could go back to-morrow and be received. I tell you this in case you think I couldn't. I have never dabbled in any transactions out here. If a Chinese bandit wants to come to Peking it's none of my business. Let him come. If you have anything against him why don't you go to the Chief of Police? Are you afraid of this man Wu?" Major Best shook his head slowly.

"No," he answered. "I can look out for myself in a tight corner, thanks. You know Chinese officials. They're as slippery as eels. I don't want to see officials, I should want to see Prince Tung."

"Prince Tung is a friend of mine," I said. "I shouldn't think of taking you there unless I know exactly what you want and you won't tell me and that's that, Best."

"Quite," the Major said. "That's fair and square. I'll tell you everything or nothing at nine o'clock to-morrow morning and you can make up your own mind then. I'm asking you something and giving nothing back, but I'm a sort who doesn't forget. Will you come at nine to-morrow?"

"Yes," I said.

The Major smiled and the watchfulness left his eyes. "Shake hands," he said. "You're a decent sort. Now dinner's ready. I mustn't keep you here too late."

CHAPTER V

MY own cook could not have prepared a better dinner. We sat at a table, beneath the glass candle lanterns, with pictures painted on the glass, and talked in a more friendly way than we have ever talked. Best raised a glass of champagne, he was doing me very well. He seemed anxious to repay me by his hospitality for something he did not care definitely to express.

"I give you the East, young fella — the Far East," he said. "And you know what that means because you and I have lived in it — the only place in the world where a man can stand on his own two feet — the only place where things are moving. Who was it who called it 'The Tinder Box of Asia?' I've got a better name for it, the Powder Magazine of the World. One spark and it goes bang. We're sitting on a powder keg now."

"I've heard all that before, but don't you think the powder's rather wet?" I asked. "It sputters but it never quite goes off."

The Major refilled my glass. His face was redder

and his cold eyes were dancing. He was not particularly attractive now that he had finished his whiskey and a half bottle of champagne. He called for another bottle to be placed on the table.

"I'll wager you it will," he said. "Take our friends, the Japanese. Jolly active, serious little Johnnys — the Japanese. They know what they want. They want a ring around China. You've seen them start. They haven't finished yet. They've snapped their fingers at Europe and have jolly well gobbled up Manchuria, and now they're reaching for North China. You've seen what's happened in the last few months. They've made the Chinese army move out of Peking. North China's as good as Japan, right now, and their agents are moving into Mongolia and into Turkestan."

There was so little new in Major Best's observations that I could not understand why he was reminding me of a state of affairs quite obvious to everyone who has taken the trouble to read newspaper reports with a Chinese date line. It has always seemed to me a piece of manifest destiny, or whatever one might choose to call it, that the Japanese Empire should control China and I told Best as much.

"Furthermore," I told him, "Imperialism is not a new or even an interesting phenomenon. My country has practised it and certainly yours has. If Japan wishes to expand she is only following every other nation from the time of Babylon; furthermore, I cannot see why outsiders should be so greatly worried. I think it would be better if everyone were to recognize what is an actual fact — Japan's ability to control the mainland of Asia. I have never seen how anything is to be gained by diplomatic quibble. Japan is a world power and a growing power; we may as well admit it."

Major Best nodded. I remember now that he followed my remarks with a greater attention than I thought they deserved.

"Quite," he said. "Oh, quite. You and I are realists, young fella, but this method of expansion — there are two schools of thought. Those are what worry me to-night. There is the school of peaceful and the school of militant expansion — the ronin school shall we call it? The disciples of both these schools are rather clashing just now over policy. That clash might make a difference here to-night."

He stopped and stirred at the champagne in his glass, watching the bubbles rush up to the surface; then he looked over the glass at me, so sharply that I was uncomfortable, with those icy, humorless eyes of his.

"Have you ever heard of a man named Takahara?" he inquired. "No? Well, Mr. Takahara is a militant Japanese. There is always some sort of an incident when this Takahara Johnny is around. He's here in Peking to-night."

"I hope he is comfortable," I said.

"Do you?" asked Major Best. "Do you really now? Well, have you thought of this, young fella? There's not a Chinese soldier in Peking to-night, but Mr. Takahara is here. The city is practically defenseless now that the army has been withdrawn. Anyone could take Peking. You and I could take it if we had a couple of thousand men."

I could not tell whether he was serious or not. I could not tell whether he was trying to convey a thought to me or simply endeavoring to make polite conversation. At any rate, he sounded fantastic enough. It was the whiskey, I decided, mixed with the champagne. It sounded like club conversations at the cocktail hour, when certain impulsive Europeans wished to hear themselves talk.

"Don't frighten me, Best," I told him. "Peking has been taken and retaken."

"Yes, young fella," said Major Best, "but it hasn't been looted for quite a while."

"Well," I said, "it won't be. The Japanese will look out for that while they as good as own it."

There was a silence when I finished. The Major had half turned his head, as though he were listening for some noise outside, and there was no trace of champagne in his voice when he answered:

44

"It doesn't matter, does it?" he said in a drawling tone which I recognized as an imitation of my own speech. "Suppose someone were to take Peking to-night?"

"That's rubbish," I said, "and you know it, Best. Why not talk about something possible?"

"Quite," said the Major, "oh quite, young fella. Nothing much has happened to Peking since that Yung Lo Johnny took it." He paused and looked at his watch. "Quite. Let's talk about something possible. Are you interested in Chinese painting, Nelson? I am just about to lay hands on some rather fine paintings, I fancy. Perhaps we'll talk of them to-morrow morning."

The watchfulness had left his eyes again. He talked for a while about Chinese art as intelligently as a connoisseur. It was a side of him which surprised me until I remembered his allusion to tomb robbing. I began to wonder if perhaps his knowledge of the money value of art might not be behind some of the mysteries of Major Best. While I was still wondering, he looked at his watch again.

"By Jove!" he said. "I didn't know it was so late. We'll have coffee in the study. I mustn't keep you too long." It was Major Best, the ladies' man, who was speaking. His maneuvre was almost transparently amusing. Now that dinner was over, it was quite clear that Major Best wished to be rid of me.

The atmosphere had changed, giving me a definite conviction that Major Best was politely and rather impatiently waiting for me to go, that he had other things to do that night, now he had obtained what he wished from me. He no longer looked at me curiously, his restlessness was growing. I had an impression that everything he had said up to then had a plan behind it, but now his conversation was desultory and careless. Even his servants seemed to share that wish to be rid of me. The whole place was waiting for me to finish my coffee and to go. It was so clear that I took a malicious pleasure in delaying my departure for a while. I lighted my cigar and brought the conversation back again to pictures. Where had the Major picked up this love for painting? Did he have any pictures to show me? Did he have any pictures to sell?

The Major was inattentive, almost discourteous, in his answers. I could hear the crickets calling. The whole place was coolly and impersonally waiting.

"Perhaps I'd better go," I said at length. "Are you expecting a caller?"

"Oh, no!" said the Major. "Jolly well not, but it is getting latish, isn't it? To-morrow morning at nine then? Good night, young fella!"

A servant had appeared with my hat. The Major walked with me to the study door. The stars were dim above the small courtyard making the trees and the roofs beyond the courtyard wall faint shadows against the sky.

"What's that?" said the Major sharply. He nodded toward the courtyard wall. There had been a rustling in the trees, but very faint.

"The wind," I said. "No need to be so restless. I'm going Major."

The Major did not answer me directly. He was staring at the tree beyond the courtyard wall. His right hand had reached inside his coat. He stared for a moment, then withdrew his hand.

"The wind," he said. "Yes. Quite! Good night, young fella. If you'll excuse me, I won't stand on ceremony as we Chinese hosts say, eh? The boy will see you across the other court. Nine o'clock tomorrow morning then? Good night!"

As I turned I left the Major standing white in the light of the doorway, still examining the trees across the court. I shall never forget the impression I had of him then. It was an exterior impression. I may have suspected but I never could be sure of what went on behind that exterior. The pleasing impersonality of the well bred Englishman enabled him to remain a complete stranger, an impossibility for an American after a few hours acquaintance. I was glad on the whole because I did not like the man.

In that hour of early darkness certain repressions seemed to have been set free in the Major's house, as watch dogs are unchained to roam at night about estates at home. They made the Major's courtyard sinister. My footsteps clattered hollowly as the servant in his white cotton gown led me through the deserted dining room of the small outside court and the front gate. I could swear that something was walking just behind me, that something was ready to touch my shoulder. I am quite sure now that if I had whirled about suddenly I should have seen something peculiar. If I had turned then, I wonder occasionally what might have happened. It is one of those useless speculations which the mind can run over vainly on wakeful nights. I did not turn around.

The gates creaked open. The doorman and the Major's number one servant stood on the threshold calling for my ricksha coolie, who appeared at almost the same instant. I was just about to step in my man-drawn vehicle when I saw the lights of another ricksha moving up the alley. Before I knew who was in it, I knew that the Major had been lying.

"It is a caller for your Master?" I said to the Major's servant.

"No caller," the man said hastily. "The Master is expecting no one." I recognized that he was lying deliberately with the hopeful mendacity of his race, which permits a Chinese to tell a blatant untruth even though he knows his falseness will be discovered a moment later.

"There must be some mistake," I said pleasantly, for the ricksha had already halted and its puller had lowered the shafts.

Then for the first time that evening I was really startled. I could see well enough who was getting out of the ricksha, for the glow of carriage lamps encircled it with a halo of yellow light. It was Miss Joyce. I could see her green dress, yellow green in the light of the lanterns, but she did not see me until I spoke. Until I saw her I believed that I might be relied upon to be suave and immune to such surprises. I was proportionately surprised at myself to discover that a part of my character which I thought had been entirely eliminated had come back. It was some conservative instinct; it was a desire to protect which was devoid of self interest.

"Miss Joyce," I said. "What are you doing here?"

CHAPTER VI

SHE was startled when she saw me, exactly as startled as I was. We stood there eyeing each other, in front of the Major's door.

"Don't you think it's rather obvious?" she inquired. "You said I'd never dare to see the world. Well, I'm going to see it."

I moved toward her, "Don't be a fool," I said.

Miss Joyce took a step toward the door. "You're the one who is being a fool," she answered. "What difference does it make to you?"

I had no adequate reply to the question, although I knew that it made a difference.

"You don't know what you are doing," I said.

"I've read books," said Miss Joyce. "I have a rather accurate theoretical idea."

For the first time in a long while I felt genuinely angry. "Get back into your ricksha," I said. "Go back where you belong. You don't belong here."

And then she was angry too.

"You're a good one to talk," she said. "I'll ask

your advice when I need it. In the meanwhile I'll look out for myself."

"You can't," I began. "You don't know how."

She walked past me, her chin in the air.

"You don't know Best," I called after her. "Eleanor! Miss Joyce!" But she was inside. The servants had already closed the door in the wall.

We must have made a delightful exhibition for the Chinese servants and one which would doubtless be retailed in all the kitchens of Peking. I had made a fool of myself. I had lost that oriental attribute called "face" before Best's servants and before my own ricksha coolie. I walked toward the closed door with some idea of banging on it, but had the sense to check myself. My ricksha coolie was watching me indifferently but I knew that not a single gesture had escaped him. I shrugged my shoulders and told him to take me home, but I could not get the thing out of my mind. It ran through my thoughts like the patter of the boy's feet. It was not right. When we had been gone for five minutes I knew that I could not leave it that way.

"Turn back," I said to my boy. He stopped and stared at me stupidly, half unwilling to understand.

"You heard me," I said. "Turn back to Major Best's."

I had no idea what I was going to do. As it turned out, there was no need for me to do anything. When we got back in the alley I saw Eleanor Joyce standing there alone. Her ricksha was gone. She was the only living soul visible on the street. She was walking slowly, blindly, regardless of the mud and ruts.

"Stop," I said to the ricksha boy, and got out and walked toward her.

"Well," I began, "so you saw the world, Miss Joyce? Are you ready to go home?"

Then I saw that she was frightened, deathly frightened; her face was chalky even in the dark.

"Don't," she whispered, "don't."

I put my arm around her shoulders. My touch steadied her, I think. "Get into my ricksha," I said. "I'll find another at the corner. Do you want to tell me what happened?"

"No," she whispered. "No. Nothing happened. Only don't go away. Walk beside me. Take my arm."

"Perhaps I'd better have a word with Best," I suggested, "before we go."

"No," her voice came back clear and sharp and frightened. "You mustn't. Don't go there. Stay here. Please, please don't leave me. He — You mustn't go in there!"

"You know I'm not afraid of Best." I said.

She clung to me, her voice was urgent. "No," she said. "You mustn't. Take me home. Please, please take me home." And then she began to cry.

I remembered that I was to see Best at nine in the morning, and the morning would be time enough.

"Yes," I said. "I'll be glad to take you home. Don't be frightened. Don't say a word. Everything is quite all right." I walked beside the ricksha wheel and held her hand. "Don't be frightened," I said again. "Everything's all right."

Then she began to laugh.

"Stop it," I said. "Stop that. Everything's all right."

Her fingers tightened on mine.

"What made you come back?" she whispered.

"Lord knows," I said. "It doesn't matter, does it?"

She was silent for a while but I knew she felt better holding my hand and hearing me talk.

"You're wrong," she said. "It matters."

I did not want her to explain what she meant because it was none of my business, and because if I had heard from her what had happened I knew that it might make me unnecessarily angry. Besides she was in no condition to speak. Whatever had occurred had frightened her severely. I recall that it surprised me at the time that she should have been so frightened by anything that Best might do.

I found a public ricksha for myself on Hatamen Street. It was one of those conveyances that was a North China substitute for a night owl taxicab in New York, which was drawn by a ragged, hungry

53

looking coolie, who probably paid a high rental for his two wheeled carriage out of the casual fares he gathered. He represented some point close to the social bottom of China, being a sort of human horse only a few steps above the burden bearers, the water, and the night-soil carriers. His life in almost any other country or compared with any other living standards would have seemed impossible. Nevertheless, he was courteously polite. His manners reminded me that Peking had been an Imperial Capital for two dynasties, a long enough time for a trace of the meticulous manners of the Court to have left a universal impression.

I explained some of this to Eleanor Joyce, as we travelled side by side in our rickshas, toward her hotel, because it did her good to hear me talk. I spoke casually and impersonally, as though we were acquaintances who had been out for a pleasant evening.

"The Peking coolies are gentlemen," I said. "It's different in the South and in the Ports. The people there have a way of being quarrelsome, but up here they are generally well disposed. One is safe in almost any corner of this city, at any hour of the day or night. Don't think China is always dangerous."

She did not answer, but I talked on, until we trotted up a shady avenue and stopped at her hotel. I helped her out of her ricksha by the hotel steps.

She was still pale and looked very tired but her voice was steady.

"Thank you," she told me, and held out her hand. Her hand seemed to have shrunk. It was small and cold, and her self assurance was gone. She looked like a little girl who was afraid that I might scold her.

"You've been very kind," she said.

"We'll forget about to-night," I answered. "It's over, isn't it?"

She nodded and said again "Thank you very much," and then she added: "You understand things very well. We have the same instincts, the same background, haven't we?"

"What makes you think that?" I asked her.

"If we hadn't," she said, "we couldn't have talked the way we did at the party. It would not have been possible. Good night!"

I had not thought of the affair from exactly that angle, but when I did I knew what she meant. It was probably true that instinct had made me behave as I did. The desire I had to protect her had probably arisen from an unconscious realization that she had been brought up as I had been, in a similar tradition. This discovery was disturbing, because I had tried for a long time to break away from tradition. I thought I had convinced myself that tradition held all the elements of emptiness and now that I was going home through the warm darkness I was not sure. I had no definite conviction just then except about one thing. I would see Best in the morning and tell him what I thought of him. Although I knew my impulse was illogical, I knew that I would do it.

My household was waiting up for me when I got back. The interests of Chinese servants necessarily revolve around the Master's doings. The gate opened promptly. Yao hurried to help me down, so assiduously that I knew something had happened. Yao followed me to my bedroom, as he always did, to fold my clothes and to talk with me as I undressed.

"Does the Master wish anything?" he enquired.

"No," I said.

"If you will sit down," said Yao, "I will take off your shoes, and here is a letter for you, a letter from America."

He called it the "Excellent Country." I understood at once the reason for his interest, when he held out the letter. He knew well enough that money and good news, and bad, came from America; and that such a letter might have an important bearing on events for several days. It might make me morose, as other letters had, and therefore its content was logically his business and the business of every servant in the household. The corner of the envelope bore the name of my former law firm, Smythe, Higgins & Satterswaith; and Yao probably knew without my ever having told him the significance of the inscription. The letter was from old Mr. Smythe himself. I did not want to read it, but I did.

Dear Tom: We all think about you a good deal and wonder if you aren't about ready to come home. I have pointed out to you before that you were never asked to resign your partnership. It was your idea, not mine or that of any of my partners, that the circumstances demanded it. The mistake you made was negligible; anything you did was for the best interests of the firm, a fact which is now generally recognized, even by our clients. You were one of the most promising junior partners we have ever had in the office. Your partnership is still open to you and we shall be glad to consider an increase in percentages and the same seniority which would now accrue to you had you stayed in the firm for the past three years.

You have too much ability to waste your life. Anyone grows maladjusted who stays in the Orient too long. In another year you will not be able to acclimate yourself to the changes in your own country. Believe me, it is changing more rapidly than I have ever known it.

As this offer cannot stay open indefinitely, I should like to hear from you by return mail. A cable might be better. Don't be a fool. Come home.

I wrinkled the sheet between my fingers. It was a sheet of fine heavy Bond, so essential to indicate the conservatism and solidity of a corporation law firm. The sheet snapped like velum between my fingers and Yao stood looking at it, without trying to conceal his curiosity.

"It is a good letter, I hope," he said.

"It is from my old Master," I told him. "I was a servant in his household. He used to make me work day and night and he paid me very badly."

Yao looked politely interested. Doubtless he was thinking of the perquisites and the percentages which he drew as a servant in my own house, and I satisfied his curiosity.

"The old Master was very close with his expenditures," I said. "Not like me, in the least. You may take this letter and burn it." I knew that he would not burn it. I knew that he would take it out and have it read, but it did not make much difference. "You may bring me my breakfast at eight o'clock to-morrow morning." I added, "I know the hour is early for me, but I have business. And now you may turn out the lights."

I lay a while staring into the dark. A year ago Mr. Smythe's letter might have disturbed me, not at present. The idea of returning was utterly distasteful and impossible. I felt no interest in the involutions of corporation law, nor was there anything in the memories of it that held me, although I had been a bright boy once. The letter was proof enough that I had been a bright boy, in an arena where competition implied the survival of the fittest. The back offices of a New York law firm was as gruelling as any apprentice room in a Chinese city street. The hours were as long and the conditions nearly as bad. I was pleased with the letter, only because it reminded me of what I had escaped instead of its implied compliment. I wished idly that I had saved it to show to Eleanor Joyce. She said that I was finished, but the letter had not said so.

I remembered what I had decided to do, as soon as I awoke in the morning. When I opened my eyes the whole chain of events which formed my conscious life came back, just as though everything had stopped until I might be ready to go on. As usual I had no great desire to go on with anything. My one wish was to sit quietly beneath the tree by my bedroom door, to read the papers perhaps, and to translate painfully some pages from the Chinese Book of Rites. Instead I had done what I had determined never to do again. I had become involved in something which was none of my business. I dressed slowly and looked at my breakfast with distaste.

"I want the ricksha ready," I said. "I am going to go out."

What followed gave me a first hand demonstration, if I had not known it, of how news travels in Peking. Yao stood beside me, pouring out my coffee.

"Please," he said. "I would not go."

"Go where?" I said. "What are you talking about?"

There is no race as perfectly endowed with the spirit of service as the Chinese, but there is a disconcerting strength in that ability to serve. Now and then there comes a faint hint that the servant is actually the master.

"Where were you last night?" said Yao. "There is trouble there, trouble."

I never asked him how he guessed that I was going back to the Major's house but accepted his guess as part of his ability.

"What sort of trouble?" I asked.

Yao folded his hands impassively. "The hard-eyed soldier is dead," he said. I knew that he was referring to Major Best, for we all had our nicknames in the Chinese servants' quarters. I set down my coffee cup, unable for a moment to grasp the potentialities of the news.

"You're wrong," I said. "He is not dead."

"He's dead," repeated Yao. "He was shot last night while in his room of books. His servant found him at two o'clock this morning."

I pushed my chair back slowly from the table where my breakfast had been laid. I was careful to make each of my motions weary and deliberate, because I did not wish Yao to perceive how hard the news had struck me.

"Get my hat," I said.

"Please," said Yao, "it would be much better not."

"Get my hat," I replied. I was uncomfortably certain that Yao knew something more but I did not wish to risk my prestige in asking him what. The thing which was uppermost in my mind was the obvious fright of Eleanor Joyce the night before. It was distinctly possible now that her fright had something to do with the death, and not the impetuous life, of Major Best. Had she seen him dead? Had she seen him murdered? Had she — ? There was a possibility that she might have done it herself. Who had last seen Major Best alive? I wondered. Had it been I or had it been Eleanor Joyce?

CHAPTER VII

IT never occured to me until I reached Major Best's door that Yao's judgment was better than my own and that I was acting impulsively without any good reason. My legal training should have been strong enough to have kept me away that morning. It had never occurred to me to inquire how the sudden death of a British citizen might be handled in Peking under the various Treaty Laws, but I was surprised that there were no police waiting at the gate. There were no police in the little outer courtyard either. A look at the servants' faces was what told me that Yao had been right. The Major's boys were exhibiting marked evidences of a passive, hopeless sort of terror that is characteristic of China.

"I am told the Major has met with an accident," I said to Best's chief servant. "I am very sorry."

The man's face was a trifle off color. His smile indicated that he was not distressed because of the tragedy as much as because of the consequences.

"Will you show me, please?" I asked.

He nodded and led the way toward the second court.

"The Major was very well when I left," I said. "You will remember that, I hope."

"Yes," he said. "Yes, I have remembered."

"And he was alive when the lady left?"

The man shook his head. "I did not see her go out," he answered. "The Master had ordered us to go to sleep. He had said there would be no one else to come or go last night. The lady took the bar from the gate herself."

The reply did not leave much doubt that the affair was ugly. The worst I had expected had happened and I knew why I had come. It was through an impulse of my legal training. It appeared quite possible to me that Eleanor Joyce would need a lawyer before the day was over.

The bright hot sunlight of that summer morning was pouring into the Court through the dancing shadows of the tree branches, so that the grey stones were a shifting carpet of lights and shades. The door of the Major's study was open and there, close to the threshold, sprawled on his back on the tiled floor, lay Major Jameson Best, still in his white suit which seemed hardly to have been disarranged.

I took off my hat without knowing exactly why except that I had seen the gesture before in motion picture films in the presence of the dead. I had no great sense of shock or any deep feeling of grief as I saw the Major lying dead, with the lines of character already erased from his face, leaving it a peaceful, open-eyed mask. Major Best was the sort to die by violence, as surely as the tiger in the stained silk painting that hung above him. He was the sort who should have died a dozen times before under the laws of averages, and probably he should have wished nothing better than this swift and painless ending. Yet it was the first time that I had seen a foreigner murdered in his own house in Peking. Such a crime was almost unheard of and the enormity of it, and the possibility that it might happen to someone else, was in itself unsettling. Then I wondered again where the police were. I was moving nearer the study door when I got my answer. There was a footstep in the study, a gentle cough, and Mr. Moto appeared in the doorway, exactly as though he were used to such matters. His grey suit was carefully pressed. The gold fillings of his front teeth, as he bobbed and smiled, glittered richly in the sunlight. He was dusting his fingers with a white silk handkerchief.

"Good morning!" he said. "It is a very nice morning, is it not? I had hoped that you would come. Shall we step inside, perhaps, and smoke a cigarette?" He stopped to speak to the servants who were gathered behind me, sharply, in Chinese.

"Leave here," he said. "We do not wish to be disturbed."

We walked gingerly past the dead man and sat

down in the two chairs which Major Best and I had occupied the previous evening. The coffee cups and the whiskey were still on the table beside me. Mr. Moto smiled again. It was one of those devastating oriental smiles, useful in concealing the more realistic facts of life.

"This is very shocking," Mr. Moto said. "I am very, very sorry. You are surprised that I am here?"

"I thought the police would be here first," I answered. "But no, I'm not much surprised."

Mr. Moto dusted his delicate hands with a handkerchief. His dark eyes moved toward me with a birdlike intensity, and he seemed to be waiting for me to make another remark.

"I am very sorry to be mixed up with your honorable country's Secret Service," I said. "I know it is a very efficient service. Of course, I understand it could only be your country's intervention which has kept the police away so long."

Mr. Moto nodded toward me. "You are a very clever man," he said. "I am very, very glad because this is very difficult. I can rely on you to be tactful, I hope. It might be difficult if you were to talk too freely — to anyone but me."

"I understand you," I said. "There is no need to threaten me. Your people hold all the cards in North China now."

"Please," said Mr. Moto. "Please do not say it just

like that. I do not threaten, oh no, of course not. It is only that you find yourself in an affair that may grow embarrassing to everyone. I have always liked Americans. Yes. And I like you very much. We shall be good friends I hope?"

Mr. Moto's voice, speaking English with a loud and difficult intensity, made me ill at ease. His matter-of-fact repression was of a sort which I had never encountered. He sat there, smoking his cigarette, as though the dead man on the floor were nothing more than some abstract event in a chain of circumstance. It was not reassuring to know that I was a part of it.

"We are good friends, oh yes," said Mr. Moto again. "It is so nice we are good friends. I am so very, very glad. It makes everything so very nice. It makes it so that I can tell you something, and then you will tell me something if you please? You say it in a beautiful way in America. You are so frank. I shall put the cards upon the table."

"That will be very nice," I said. And Mr. Moto drew in his breath between his teeth, and raised his hand before his mouth, and let it drop again on the arm of his chair.

"My people have much to concern them lately," he went on. "We have many delicate combinations. You are clever to know that I have something to do with our Intelligence Service and I cannot imagine how you guessed. You are right in believing that this unpleasantness here has certain implications. You need not bother to — er — calculate what they are, and I hope you understand?"

"Well enough," I said. "Thank you, Mr. Moto. You are interested because I was here last night. I hope you do not think I killed Major Best?"

"Please," said Mr. Moto. "Please. Oh no, of course not!" He pointed at the dead man's head. There was no doubt as to how he had died. There was a bluish puncture in the centre of the Major's high narrow forehead.

"He died," said Mr. Moto, "while standing here in the doorway — while speaking to someone, I think, for I found this near his feet." Mr. Moto reached a hand delicately into his coat pocket and drew out a gold compact case. "A lady was talking to Major Best," he said. "There is a saying among the Secret Service men in your country, where I have had the honor to study once, that a woman always leaves something. We both know her name, of course. Are you interested, Mr. Nelson?"

I did not like the look of it, and I was shaken more than was reasonable because it indicated that Eleanor Joyce was on the verge of ruin. A few words from Mr. Moto and she would never show her face at home again. Under such circumstances there did not seem to be much use in appealing to Mr. Moto's chivalry. I pointed to the wound in Major Best's forehead.

"A large bullet did that — at least a forty-five. Yes, we both know who the lady is, but she would have used something smaller, don't you think?"

Mr. Moto turned toward me and sucked in his breath emphatically.

"In a matter like this one," he said, "it might be very useful to conceal the motive of this crime. You mean the weapon was too large for the other sex. Yet I saw you myself conversing with the lady yesterday evening. I understand that you had words with her, outside this house last night. It may have been that you came back. The Chinese police and your own nationals would be interested to hear it. Shall I tell them, Mr. Nelson?"

A slight tremor ran down my spine but I kept my voice steady. "You talk and I'll talk too. I'll tell you anything I know, if that is what you want," I said. Mr. Moto nodded.

"That is very, very nice — if you will be so kind," he said. "You tell me, please, what words were spoken last night when you dined with Major Best. You tell me everything you saw. Exactly, if you please."

I did not like his tone but it did not seem the time to tell him so. Instead, there was only one thing

68

to do. I described the evening with Major Best. Mr. Moto sat listening, his face preoccupied and intent. He was trying to piece something together. I did not know exactly what.

"The man's name was Wu Lo Feng," I said.

"Yes," said Mr. Moto. "Now I understand. That is exactly what I wished to know. I did not know the name. Thank you very much. May I ask you one more question? Could anyone have overheard your talk last night?" He waved his hand toward the open doorway, across the sunny Court. "Someone, for instance, in the trees beyond the wall? You say there was a rustling in the trees?"

"Perhaps," I said. "It doesn't matter, does it?"

Mr. Moto looked at me impersonally and then his glance moved to the figure of Major Best.

"It was not possible — " the softness of Mr. Moto's voice, the slow careful stress which he put on each syllable, made his question deliberately emphatic. "Think — think very carefully, if you please, that the Major mentioned someone else, a countryman of mine?"

"What was his name?" I asked.

"Takahara." Mr. Moto's voice had dropped almost to a whisper. "Takahara was the name."

"Yes," I told Mr. Moto. "Best asked me if I knew him. He said he was the sort who is in the centre of trouble. I'd never heard of him."

Mr. Moto leaned closer to me and raised his hand before his mouth, so that I might not be contaminated by his breath.

"Please," he said, in that same soft voice, "I think it would be better if you forget his honorable name. That is my affair. You have asked me if these things matter. If they do, I shall be very, very sorry for you. Yes! Very, very sorry!"

"Moto?" I asked him, "what do you mean by that?"

"Only this," said Mr. Moto smoothly, "I am very sorry you should have been inconvenienced. Very, very sorry. You must forget, please, everything that you have heard. I know that I may rely on you for that. Our friend here was not killed by a pistol shot. He was killed by a bolt sent from a crossbow, so that there was no sound of a shot. The Chinese crossbows are very nice. You have seen them on sale no doubt? But now, I must not keep you any longer." Mr. Moto rose and I rose also. "This matter will be arranged quietly, do not fear. Many things happen here quietly. I only ask you to forget — all names, everything. And now good morning, Mr. Nelson! Sometime I shall call on you, I hope so very much, and we shall drink whiskey together like good Americans. Ha, ha! And have a talk like friends. You have been very nice. Please excuse everything. Good morning!"

Mr. Moto turned his attention again to the body of Major Best, but just as I was starting away he called me back.

"Excuse me, please," he said. "Here is something I have forgotten. Will you return it please?" And he handed me the gold compact case. "You see, I trust you, Mr. Nelson. You have been very, very nice."

I thanked him, although I felt quite sure that Mr. Moto trusted no one. Nevertheless, that last gesture of his filled me with deep relief. That tableau of the study, of the dead man, and of the glinting gold filled teeth of Mr. Moto, had implications the more disturbing because I could not guess them. Mr. Moto's businesslike adroitness was something which I did not wish to see again. My mind went back to Eleanor Joyce, now that I was holding her compact in my hand. My mind went back just as I had turned back to her, instinctively, the night before — in spite of my doctrine of broad tolerance which I had thought that China had taught me.

"Mr. Moto," I said, and he looked up patiently and intently, although I knew that he wished that I would go, "I should like to be reassured about just one thing."

"Yes?" said Mr. Moto. "One thing? Yes?" He had never seemed so delicate as he did when I stood there looking down at him, a miniature of a man, as small as the gardens and the dwarfed trees of his island.

"I'd like your definite word," I said, "that Miss Joyce will not be involved in this. It was a mistake — her being here last night."

"Of course," said Mr. Moto heartily. "Yes, of course — only a mistake. We can be gentlemen, of course. You need not worry about Miss Joyce. This is not a lady's business. Oh no! Not at all. I shall manage now, I think."

"Thanks," I said, and I found that I actually believed him. "Thank you very much."

"And now," said Mr. Moto again, imperviously polite, "I must not keep you any longer, but please, may I give you some advice as a friend? I should go back to your house. It must be very comfortable — you have such very good taste — and think no more about this. Remember only that you had a little dinner with Major Best the evening before he died and that it is very sad. Remember nothing else. I hope you understand?"

I understood and we shook hands.

"It's all over as far as I'm concerned," I said. "I'm not a fool and I don't meddle."

CHAPTER VIII

I HAD not realized how much the interview with Mr. Moto had tired me until I was in my ricksha again, moving down the street. Then I took out my handkerchief and mopped my forehead, and my forehead was moist and clammy in spite of the warm sun. The reaction from that conversation was settling heavily upon me and with it a sense of deep relief. It is not so often in life that one has a second chance. Contrary to all my principles of not interfering in the course of events, I had deliberately involved myself in the adventures of a girl whom I hardly knew. I had acted quixotically, and China is no place for quixotic action, since the consequences are too unfathomable.

I had stepped, and she had stepped, close to the brink of a secret that had sent a man to his death. The shadows of that secret had been close about us for a while, and now by great good fortune those shadows had disappeared. I had stood by her and I had saved her perhaps from unpleasant consequences and now the slate was clean. I could go back to my life as it had been and she could go back to hers. It was like the dance of the evening before, when we had been close together for a moment — and now the dance was over.

"Well," I said to myself, "that's over and it doesn't matter, does it?"

But it was not as easy as I had thought to feel that it did not matter, because something was all around me. Something had brushed by and had touched my shoulder. It had to do with a bandit in blue coolie clothes and the hard-eyed Major Best whose eyes were glazed forever, with an unknown but certainly disagreeable person named Mr. Takahara, and the intrigue of Japan. All the stories and the gossip which one hears in China in these days: of Japanese agents working mole-like in the dark, of sudden death, of bribery and corruption and of manufactured incidents, all had a new significance to me. I tried to set my thoughts in order, but I could not. I could not rid my memory of the body of Major Best sprawled on the study floor. He had died because he knew something. I was sure of that. Nor could I escape the vision of Mr. Moto, cool and professional. It was none of my business but I wondered how Mr. Moto had heard the news, when a crossbow shot made no sound.

Then my thoughts were running along another entirely useless channel, since Eleanor Joyce was out of this affair, I wondered, if things had been different how I should have acted, well or badly. Probably badly.

"Well," I said to myself again. "That's over and it doesn't matter, does it?"

Yet even then I must have realized that it was not over. Once you touch a thing like that — once you get in the way of something, by all the laws of human action there is a different sort of ending. A question of Mr. Moto's came back to me, which had not impressed me at the time.

" 'Could one have overheard your talk last night? Someone, for instance, in the trees beyond the wall? . . . You have asked me if these things matter. If they do, I shall be very, very sorry for you. Yes! very, very sorry!' "

Though there was nothing that pointed at danger, yet one could not be sure, because nothing was sure in those days.

CHAPTER IX

THE situation which I am trying to describe is an indefinable and difficult matter, because it is a mood. I am trying to piece together a series of events following my meeting with Mr. Moto, events which started as small matters in themselves and ended in something close to climax. Now as I look back on them, I believe I always had a subconscious sense of something dangerous impending, for there is a part of one's mind when it is aroused that is suspicious without reason — that never entirely sleeps. The difficulty is that the way I reacted to these events implies a certain knowledge of China, of the deviousness and the indirectness of its life, and this makes it a hard matter to explain.

China and Peking that morning were closing about me in small gossamer meshes, so guilelessly as to be beyond accurate perception. I was on my way home, on the broad modern street again, which passes the South Wall of the Forbidden City. All the appurtenances of the place were beginning to take on a jewel like glitter in the growing heat of the sun. The pink walls had a warmer hue, totally different from the icy pink of winter. Waves of heat radiated silkily from the yellow tiles. The white marble bridges over the outer moat sparkled in intricate, lacelike patterns. The cedars above the wall of the Tai Miao, where the Emperors once communed with the spirits of their royal dead, gave the only touch of color which was cool. I felt my utter insignificance as I saw that glow of color. I understood why the Chinese dwelt within walled courts, through my own desire to be again inside my walls, which would shut out symbolism and mystery. I remembered the first time that I had set eyes on Peking streets and recalled that baffling impression of utter unfamiliarity, that lack of any basis for comparison with my own world, which every scene had presented. In the lapse of time between that first encounter and the present I had thought that I had learned something, but now I knew that I had not, and that I never would. The minutiae and the complexities of the Chinese mind, as represented by that city, were too great to be mastered, too diffuse ever to permit an accurate conclusion. Any generalization might be partially correct and be, at the same time, entirely wrong. In spite of the bright sun, I was like someone wandering in the dark.

When Yao stood at my door to meet me he no longer seemed like an individual whose traits I knew almost as well as my own. Instead of being able to associate him with his stupidities and his weaknesses, he became to my imagination a composite of all his race. His face had that placid, exasperating patience of China. The cynicism and materialism, so refined as to be nearly spiritual, the bluntness and the delicacy of perception, the abjectness and the vanity, the bravery and the cowardice, the loyalty and the deceit — all those eternal contradictions of China were printed on it. He was as difficult to construe as a page of Chinese characters whose ideographs shift elastically in accordance with the reader's own thoughts. Yao followed me to my room and stood without speaking while I sat down behind my red lacquer desk.

"What do you want?" I asked.

Yao folded his hands in his white cotton sleeves. "My mother in the country has been taken dangerously ill," he said. "I must go to her at once."

Yao knew, as I did, that his sick mother was like the American office boy's excuse to see the ball game. The illness of his mother was a convention for saving face and a delicate method of avoiding painful explanations. Yao was announcing conventionally that he was about to quit my service after three quiet, profitable years beneath my roof. I knew that he would never give an explanation, but I was certain that something had happened that very morning to make him reach such a decision. His patience and passivity, and his self-effacing quietness, conveyed a message to me, for I had seen the same expression on other Chinese faces. Yao was afraid and he could not entirely hide his fear. There was even a contagion in his state of mind that shook my placidity and self control. I wished to ask him what he was afraid of, even though I knew he would not answer.

"The illness of my parent is all that could take me away," he answered. "It is the only devotion above the devotion to my Master."

"Very well," I said. "Since you are going to your sick mother, who I hope will soon recover, have you brought someone to take your place?" My question appeared to hurt him.

"I could not do otherwise," he answered, "after serving you for so long. My cousin is coming to take my place this afternoon. He is a most reliable man. He will serve you honestly."

"I have no doubt," I said, "but I do not desire your cousin." My reaction was instinctive because Yao's mysterious behavior made anything connected with him mysterious. If he was afraid, his cousin would be also.

"My Master does not trust me?" Yao inquired.

"I did not say that," I told him. "I simply said

that I do not desire your cousin. You may bring me your accounts at luncheon time. What are you waiting for? You may go."

But Yao still waited.

"Pu, the curio dealer, is here with the pictures," he said.

At this point my patience, which I had always striven to maintain in the oriental manner, wore thin and snapped.

"You fool!" I said to him. "How dare you introduce a merchant here when you have upset my household? I did not ask for him. Send the man away."

I should have known that it is generally useless to swim against the current of a servant's desire. Before I had finished speaking, Pu the curio dealer with his blue cloth bundles, his wispy grey mustaches and his blue cotton gown, was smiling and bowing in the open door. Pu and I had done small pieces of business before and, like most residents of Peking, I had my following of Chinese antiquaries who came occasionally to my house. I had grown to realize long ago that they seldom brought anything of rare artistic value. The agents of foreign dealers and of rich collectors had the first selection, so that what was left was second rate. I tolerated the dealers more for the purpose of conversation than for buying, and as a man Pu was interesting; he had a finesse of touch and perception that on the whole was fascinating under the proper circumstances.

"I am engaged in other business," I said. "I cannot see you to-day."

I might have known that the old man would ignore my remark. Before I could say anything further he had knelt theatrically at my feet and had pulled a scroll from one of his cloth bundles.

"Only a moment," he said, in a voice like honey and rippling water. "See what I have saved for the Master! He is the first one to see it."

"I said that I was engaged," I began and then I stopped.

I had a good reason to stop when I caught a glimpse of the scroll that he was unrolling, for I realized even when I had seen a little of it that I was experiencing one of those moments which are talked of but which are seldom known. I was looking at a work of art as distinguished and as rare as a Botticelli in another incarnation. It was one of those scroll paintings, made to be unrolled a little at a time, and intended for leisurely contemplation. It was a series of landscapes and pastoral scenes that moved and changed, as China changes on a journey; from mountains to valleys, from valleys to rivers, from farms to villages and temples. No museum piece that I had ever seen compared with it. The delicacy of the brush strokes and the verity of the color gave one the illusion of living inside that scroll, and of experiencing almost physically each phase of the moving scene. The technique was simple, so naïvely uncomplicated that it was not difficult to attribute the painting to one of the earlier dynasties, some part of the Sung I could believe. It was in beautiful preservation, in spite of its great age. It must have been kept since the 12th Century, in a succession of rich men's strong boxes. It must have invariably been handled with reverence and respect. It was easy to watch in silence as the scenes unrolled themselves between the dealer's nimble fingers. When the scroll was finished, he looked up at me ingratiatingly.

"Have I not done well?" he asked.

It seemed impossible that such a picture should be lying there on my floor. There was no use in pretending that I was not impressed, for the old man had read my thoughts. His watery eyes were watching every muscle and every change in my expression.

"Where did you get that?" I asked.

Pu moved his hands resignedly and smiled. "It is a great treasure, is it not?" he said. "It was given into my care by a friend who wishes it to be in safe hands. He realizes that nothing is safe now, in his hands or in the hands of any of his countrymen."

He paused, still watching me. The answer had been evasive as I knew it would be.

"Why should it not be safe in Chinese hands?" I said.

He smiled up at me, still kneeling on the floor. "Surely you understand," he said. "Times in the Provinces are very uncertain. Since the army has been moved in accordance with the last demands of Japan, a wise man takes precautions. Property is no longer safe in Peking. Silver can be buried but not a picture."

My mind was still on the sight I had seen. The painting of the cliffs and trees had been familiar. While the old man was talking my mind went over the list of the better known Sung artists. The scroll might have been a work of the Emperor Hwei-tsung. If this was so, it might have come from a Temple chest or from the hands of some connection of the Manchu dynasty. As I say, the picture distracted my attention from the old man's words.

"I have just heard it said that Peking is not safe," I answered. "I do not understand just why."

The old man's voice was mild and careless.

"What has the Master heard?" he asked. His voice was careless but his eyes were not. For some reason he seemed anxious for my answer. So anxious that I did not give it, and instead I asked a question in return.

"Have you brought this picture for sale?" I asked him.

He nodded. It almost seemed, although it was incredible, as if he were not interested in the price.

"If you wish," he explained, "as I am not the owner, I can only transmit your offer to my friend. There is one thing very sad. The picture was to have been offered to-day to the Englishman, Major Best. Is it not very sad? I am sorry because the Major was a friend of yours and one whom I greatly admired." Again his eyes were studying my face and I knew that he had seen my surprise. The old man had lived by his wits too long for me to be his equal.

"Yes," I said. "It is very sad."

"The Major may have spoken to you of the pictures, among other things, last night?" His voice was casual again but his eyes were not.

"No," I said. "He did not." I believe he knew that my answer was not accurate. I did not recall until I had given it that last night the Major had talked of pictures.

"The great soldier was generally a quiet man," old Pu remarked. "You have asked me where the picture came from. One generally does not betray these confidences, but we are old friends and I shall tell you the name of the man who brought it to me, although his name will mean nothing to you. His name is," Pu lowered his voice, "Wu Lo Feng, a stranger in our city. You have never heard his name?"

But he knew that I had heard it. I was helpless

beneath his attention, and conscious of my barbaric crudity.

"Only once, long ago, I heard the name," I said. I was quite sure that he knew that I was speaking an untruth. He was smiling, but an invisible veil had dropped over the brightness of his eyes and he reached for the picture and put it back in the bundle.

"To-morrow," he said. "I will come again. To-day I merely wanted you to see."

"Wait," I said. "Will you not leave the picture?"

"Gladly, if it were mine." His answer was courteous, regretful. "I do not dare to because it is another's. But to-morrow I shall bring it back. I just wish to show it to an American lady who may buy — Miss Joyce." His eyes met mine again and dropped away, but not before he saw my expression change — and I knew that it had changed.

Then it seemed to me that he was in a hurry to go. It was one of the few times that I had ever known a Chinese curio dealer to be in a hurry. He bowed and walked away with Yao, along the garden path toward the gate. For a moment I sat looking after him, aware that something had been wrong, without being able to specify what. I had become accustomed to the amenities and courtesies of Chinese conversation, all of them as accurate as the openings of a game of Chess. I had talked long enough to dealers to know the patterns of bargaining, to realize that this time the conventions had been different. My intuition was strong enough to tell me that he had wanted something of me. He had not wished to sell the picture. He had wished the sight of it to take me off my guard. He had asked me if I had heard of Wu Lo Feng. I remembered Major Best's words on the subject.

"My life wouldn't be worth tuppence if he knew I knew him."

The antique dealer had come there to elicit a piece of information. He had deliberately woven three names into the talk as he had watched me. I could not tell why and that was what disturbed me most. Moreover, he must have found out what he wished or he would have been in no hurry to go.

I sat for a minute or two, thinking, vaguely surprised that I should be so disturbed; for restlessness was growing within me, sending out shoots and tendrils like an unhealthy weed. The shade of Major Best had followed me home. He was there beside me and I could not shake him off, but what worried me most was the mention of Eleanor Joyce's name, and Pu had read my worry. There was no doubt of that.

Even so, I think I should have sat there quietly, worried but not stirred into any definite action, waiting, as I had liked to wait, for events to take their course, if I had not opened the drawer of my red lac-

86

quer desk. I did this half mechanically, following a habit of a morning's routine, and the pages of my manuscript lay there, but not in the even pile in which I had left them. Then I opened the other drawers where my slender correspondence was kept, and again I had a sense that the order was not right.

"Yao," I shouted. "Have you been inside my desk?"

"No," said Yao. "Not I—a friend of yours, who came last night. Your friend from Japan, Mr. Moto of course, who said you had asked him to read what you had written."

It was the effrontery of Mr. Moto's that aroused me. There was something behind his interest that came close to making me afraid. I took my hat, without a word, and walked out to the gate.

"The Great Hotel," I said. I was going to see Miss Joyce, if only because Mr. Moto had advised me to stay at home.

CHAPTER X

IT is strange, as one grows older, how mercilessly one becomes enmeshed in the material side of life, so that in spite of one's better judgment one begins to evaluate by externals. I suppose that I had begun to reach that stage, for I found when I evaluated everything I knew about Eleanor Joyce that all my discoveries had been purely external. Except for a moment when she had been afraid, in front of the Major's house, she had been an abstraction, carefully hidden behind dress and convention. She had said we had the same traditions and our tradition was largely one which dealt with façades. Her sitting room at the hotel was a façade. It had all the proper bits of Chinese bric-a-brac and all the suitable books which might pertain to an interesting young woman who had a smattering of intellectuality.

Eleanor Joyce herself seemed to have retired behind a façade; she was dressed in a white piqué skirt and a pullover. I noticed that her color was not right. Her lips were too crimson; her cheeks had been too patently rouged.

"I'm glad you've come. It's been terrible," she said.

"Yes," I said. "Rather!"

"Well, it doesn't seem to have affected you much," she replied. "Excitement is rather becoming to you, as a matter of fact."

Without wishing to frighten her, there was one thing I wished to be sure of. I tiptoed to the hall door and opened it quickly, but no one was outside.

"I'm sorry," I explained. "I wanted to be sure that we were alone."

She laughed, but her laugh was not quite steady. "I am very much flattered," she answered. "What is the matter? Aren't you going to tell me?"

I did not know exactly how to begin. I sat down and looked at her for the moment. Now that I had mentioned it, we seemed very much alone indeed. Her brown eyes were wide, attentive and honest.

"We seem rather thrown together," I said. "I've had you a little on my mind to-day."

She laughed again unsteadily. "Is that all?" she asked.

"Not quite," I told her. "You should learn to be more careful about your personal belongings, and not to strew them around quite so much. You left your gold compact at Major Best's last night."

She sat up a trifle straighter.

"Who told you that?" she asked.

I admired her poise in a way, I had thought she would have been frightened.

"A mutual friend of ours," I said. "A Japanese named Mr. Moto. Do you remember him? I had a talk with him this morning."

"Did you?" There was a coolness in her voice which I had not noticed before. "So did I. Mr. Moto called on me here this morning."

I was not surprised because I should not have expected less of him. "What did he want?" I asked.

"He wanted me to tell him exactly what happened last night," she said. "I told him all he needed to know."

"That's exactly why I'm here," I said. "I think you'd better tell me too."

"Why?" she asked. "Why should I?"

"I wish I could tell you exactly," I told her. "I believe we know something which is interesting to someone. There is something which the Major knew and someone believes he told it. I'll tell you why I think so. I have been followed all day to-day, and now, just before I came to see you, a picture dealer called at my house, not to sell me anything but to ask me questions. I'm not altogether a fool, Miss Joyce. I was the junior partner of a law firm, a trial lawyer, before I came out here. The work teaches you observation, and dealing with Chinese teaches you more than that. There is something — something which isn't right. I should rather like to know what it is. I'm thinking of you as much as myself. Will you tell me exactly what happened?"

She was looking at me for almost the first time since I had known her. Her look was not impersonal. She stretched her hand toward me, palm upward.

"Will you give me my compact, please?" she asked me.

I took it out of my pocket and handed it to her.

"How did you know I had it?" I asked.

"Because I've changed my opinion of you since yesterday," she said. "If you knew that I had left that compact, I knew that you would see that it got back to me. You've been rather kind to me — for no very good reason. I owe you a good deal already. You needn't have come back last night. A good many men I know wouldn't have." She smiled at me almost shyly. "Well, Eleanor Joyce pays her debts. That's why I'm not going to tell you anything. There is no reason for your being dragged into this any further. It would not be fair. I don't suppose most women are really fair, but I try to be. If I've done a foolish thing there is no reason why I should not take my own medicine — just as a man would — just as you would, I think. It isn't that I don't want to tell you because there's nothing that I'd rather do. I'm rather frightened now. I'm rather lonely, staying here all day, thinking and thinking. But I won't tell you anything except this: I'm not out here entirely for pleasure. There is no reason for you to worry about me, none at all. I'm not the sort who gets into trouble and runs for help. You mustn't worry about what anyone says of me. There will be talk enough, I suppose. I can shut my eyes and hear everybody talking — "

"No," I said. "There won't be much talk, not about you, I think. There were plenty of good reasons, if you'll excuse my saying so, for Major Best to die, besides the real reason. As far as you and I are concerned, we're caught in something — whether we like it or not — "

Eleanor Joyce sat up straighter.

"I may be. You're not. Please don't ask me to tell you anything because I won't. And there's one thing more. We should not be seen together. I'm sorry, because it has occurred to me to-day that we might have rather a pleasant time and now we can't. You must keep away from me as though I were poison ivy. I'm sorry, but I think you'd better be going now."

It seemed to me I had never known who she was, although that is a clumsy way of describing something which is impossible to put into words. Those rare moments of rapprochement between two human beings are generally beyond analysis. She was suddenly a person of flesh and blood, endowed with character, imbued with generosity. Her character was almost tangible and it made me ashamed of myself, because I had come there to see her mainly for selfish reasons and she had been thinking of me. She had said that Eleanor Joyce always paid her debts.

"Has it occurred to you that two might handle this better than one?" I began.

But she stopped me. "You can't talk me out of it," she said. "It is no use trying. I have as strong a will as you have, probably stronger. I've got to go through this entirely alone. You understand that, don't you?"

And in a way I did understand it. I arose and held out my hand. "All right," I said. "But you can't arrange things as easily as that. Whether you like it or not, we're both in this together. If you don't want me here now, I'll go but it won't be permanent."

"Why do you say that?" she asked me quickly.

"Because it is fatality," I told her. "We've been caught in a current, I hope a very small one, but when you're caught in a current you can't help it. I've been writing a book about it."

"I don't agree with you," she said. Her hand gripped mine frankly, almost like a man's.

"But it's so," I told her. "Will has very little to do with anything. There's something else inside us that makes the will play tricks. If you and I like each other we'll see each other, whether we want or not."

"I don't believe it," she said again.

93

"I'm afraid that doesn't matter," I answered. "And you can't help my looking out for you, whether you want it or not. I'll be seeing you. Good bye!"

I was two steps away from the door when she called me back.

"Wait," she said. "You're not angry with me, are you?"

"No," I said. "On the contrary, I wish I'd known a girl like you five years ago."

"I'm glad you said that," she said quite soberly. "It's so hard to tell what you really think. You have a poker face and half the time you're acting. You're a complicated sort of person."

"Not basically," I said. "All human beings are rather simple basically. You're simple. I'm simple."

"But not when we're together," she said. "Good bye."

CHAPTER XI

IT was true what she said. When we were together things were complicated. I was disturbed because she sent me away, and that in itself was illogical enough. I know now that the current which had drawn us together was moving me without my own volition, but I did not know it then. My only reaction was a desire then not to be alone. I wanted to be with people and to have my own thoughts dulled by the anesthetic of talk. That was why I went to the Club, after seeing Eleanor Joyce, simply as a way of retreating from something which seemed to be following me and which seemed to be all around me.

The Club turned out to be an adequate answer to what I wanted. There was nothing mysterious or subtle inside it, scarcely a touch of the East about it, which was probably its chief attraction in that distant city. The Club was predominantly British, a tribute to that colonizing ability of its founders which has enabled them to make any British outpost, from the wilds of Canada to the rubber plantations of Singapore, the same as any other. The dark woodwork had a hint of Victorian manners. The faces were controlled. There was a sense of the Anglo-Saxon race standing together, a somewhat out-of-date sense of empire, which had been voiced by Kipling once. The security of manifest Nordic destiny was still there, and it was singularly peaceful to me that noon. I was sorry that I had ever left that security. I did not wish to go back to my Chinese house.

It was getting toward luncheon at the time I arrived and the tables in the bar room were filling up. Jim Greenway from the Imperial Shensi Bank was there, and the manager of the cable company and Captain Clough from the marines. The Chinese bar boys were hurrying from table to table with trays weighted with soda bottles and whiskey. There was a sound of shaking dice.

"Boy," voices were shouting. "Boy," with the same assurance as though the Anglo-Saxon was still the dominant race in the Orient. Several people called to me when I came in. Greenway waved an arm to me. Clough pointed to a chair, and I joined them.

"Boy," I found myself calling. "Scotch and soda, Boy."

Clough, who was heavy and methodical, continued exactly where he had left off.

"And I say, under the circumstances everybody had better carry a gun," he said. "This thing is disturbing. Tom, have you got a gun?"

"No," I answered. "Why?"

"He's the sort who never hears anything," Greenway said. "Haven't you heard the news?"

"No," I answered. "What?" But I guessed what the news would be.

"Best killed himself last night."

"What? Killed himself?" My surprise was genuine enough.

"Found dead with a forty-five automatic in his hand," said Captain Clough. "It's all regular enough. We all know Best. He probably had reasons enough to kill himself. But then!"

"But what?" I said.

Captain Clough drew a deep breath. "What I've been saying. I don't like it. Best wasn't the suicide kind. You know what I mean when I say it. There's a sort of man who just won't kill himself, no matter what sort of a mess he's in. I know Best."

My hand was unsteady as I lifted up my glass. It occurred to me that Mr. Moto had done very well. He was hushing matters up exactly as he had promised.

"You never can tell," I said. "Things happen that way sometimes. I'm sorry, but then perhaps it's just as well."

"Perhaps," said Clough. "But just the same I advise everybody outside the Legation compound to carry a gun. I've always advised it. I've got a thirty-eight in my bag outside. I'll lend it to you if you like."

His advice was exactly what I should have expected. The Captain was of the alarmist type who believes that the Orient is full of hidden enemies. I told him so, and everybody laughed.

"Besides," I said. "What should I do with a revolver? I've never handled one in my life." My confession was a shocking one to the Captain. As shocking as though I had told a missionary that I was an atheist.

"You're not serious, are you Tom?" he said.

"Yes," I answered. "But it doesn't matter, does it?"

The talk moved into other channels after that. The East is a hard place, too callous for the news of death to disturb its equanimity. By the time luncheon was finished and we were seated about a bridge table the shadowy career of Major Best was in the past. The Captain's talk about firearms was nearly all that lingered in my mind. My mind was on revolvers, as the cards clicked on the table. It was true I had never handled one, but I had an accurate idea as to how it was done. My cards were very good that afternoon and we four played steadily, aware that time made no great difference. When we finished Captain Clough owed me thirty dollars and I thought of the revolver again. I had an impulse as I thought of it.

"Give me your gun and I'll call it square," I said.

That was how it happened that I left the Club carrying a revolver in the side pocket of my coat with cartridges in the chamber, for the first time in my life. There was nothing deliberate about it. I had no real sense of danger. The Club was filling up again for the cocktail hour before dinner.

"Did you hear about Best?" they were saying. "He killed himself. A bad sort. Always knew he would."

I could hear the word "Best" over the tinkling of the glasses. Mr. Moto had done very well. The end of Major Best was taken for granted already and without question by everyone except my bridge opponent, Captain Clough.

"Best," they were saying. "Best! A forty-five automatic in his hand and a bullet through his head. Well, one has to stop somewhere."

Everyone knew the story by then. It was already becoming enlarged and distorted by the grapevine telegraph of gossip. Everyone knew that Best had killed himself, for some reason which had better not be mentioned, although everyone was busy supplying a reason. I could hear their voices chattering in my memory all the way home, rising above the street noises of Peking.

"Best," they were saying. "Well it couldn't have been different. He had to leave Shanghai. There was something in the army. There was something up at Kalgan . . . crooked . . . yellow . . . something."

For the first time I felt sorry for his memory, because, I suppose, there is an instinctive respect for the dead. The memory of the cool-eyed Major had been wronged mercilessly and efficiently and slandered when he could not answer back. I could see Mr. Moto working in the Major's study, changing a murder to a suicide, studiously and conscientiously. It was an upsetting and a ghoulish picture which I could not put aside. Now that the dusk was coming on, the uncertainty of all the events which had transpired in the last twenty-four hours were given an odd and new perspective, becoming magnified and distorted like shapes seen through rippling water. Suppose, I was thinking, that I should be killed, would Mr. Moto arrange it too that I had killed myself? In spite of the noises on the street, I had a sense of silence and of tenseness as though everything were waiting. It may have been premonition. I believe in premonition now.

For the first time that I could remember the red gate of my wall did not open after my ricksha stopped before it. My boy had to bang against it with the great iron ring and to shout shrilly for attention. For a moment or so his clamor seemed like the futility of all human endeavor. The clang of the iron ring rose through the warm close air with his voice, up toward the deepening violet of the sky. The dusky shadows seemed to fall like nets to catch the sound and out of the shadows came the nervous staccato chant of locusts and crickets. It was a sound that was indescribably sad and mocking; then the yard coolie opened the door so slowly and reluctantly that I grew angry.

"What is the matter here?" I asked him. "Where is Yao?" The man was a dull witted member of the human burden bearing class. It took him a moment to find a suitable answer. He wagged his head nervously, opened his mouth and closed it.

"He is gone," he said. "His mother is very ill. So are the parents of the cook and the assistant cook. They regretted that they must leave. There is only myself here now."

Unless one has lived in the Orient, it is hard to understand how utterly such disregard of the employer's status and comfort might shock one. At any rate, it made me indignant, to the point of violence.

"You mean to say," I demanded, "that there is no one here to prepare my dinner?" I turned to the ricksha boy. "Go," I said. "Get some people to prepare my dinner. Find someone at once."

"Who shall I find," he asked, "Master?"

"Anyone," I said. "Don't argue with me, you turtle's egg. Do you think I am going to do without my dinner? Do you think I am going to get it myself?"

My last question showed him, perhaps, that things

had come to a serious pass, because he hurried away. I was still deeply shocked as I walked through my blue and white garden; I had thought mistakenly that my servants were devoted, although I should have known much better. I walked quickly into the second court, turning over the situation in my mind, nearly oblivious to everything around me. Yet I remember that the shade trees over the wall were growing a very dark green in the dusk, making the whole place dusky green, like the depths of a shadowy pool, and I recall that incessant chirping of the crickets. The sound was nervous and out of key. I walked toward the room that opened off my bedroom, the room where my red lacquer desk and my books were, that I used for dressing and writing. It was almost dark inside. I paused at the door to grope for the antiquated light switch, for electrical appliances are not modern in Peking. I was half inside and half out of the door when I contrived to switch on the light, with my head turned sideways against the frame of the open doorway. It is singular how accurately one can reconstruct such small details and yet what a margin of error there still exists in recollection.

The light went on, and I was just about to move inside — I was just turning my head, in fact, when two things happened almost instantaneously. Something went buzzing so close by my forehead that I could almost feel its impact. There was a plop of something that had imbedded itself in the door frame, and at the same instant there was a sound across the court, a snapping sound like a string pulled on a base viol so hard that it strikes the wood. I knew what had happened. Though my mind appeared to accept these events deliberately, my body did not. My body had given a lurch to get inside the door. My hand in a spasm of panic was switching out the light but my body in its haste had forgotten the high Chinese door sill. I tripped over it, and the next instant I had fallen flat into the room. Then I was drawing myself up on my hands and knees cautiously, noiselessly, like a hunted animal. In the midst of all this motion my mind was running smoothly. I knew exactly what had happened. A bolt from a crossbow had whizzed by my head, not a quarter of an inch away from it. I had heard the twang of the string across the court. If I had not moved my head at that instant, I should have been in front of the door as dead as Major Jameson Best.

CHAPTER XII

I SUPPOSE I must have been afraid, but I was still moving instinctively. I was crouching just inside the door, with my shoulder against my red lacquer desk; goose flesh was rising and falling in waves up and down my back. I knew that I was still in danger, that the thing was not over yet, that whoever had shot had seen me fall. Whoever it was might be coming into the courtyard at any moment to find me crouching inside the door. Then my hand was in the side pocket of my coat, gripping that revolver. My fingers were shaking until they touched the metal; then I was holding it in my hand quite steadily. I remember being surprised that I seemed to be intuitively familiar with it. I was holding the revolver ready and listening, as though I expected some sound that was inevitable. I heard it half a minute later.

There were footsteps in the dusk outside. I wished to peer round the door frame but I didn't. The steps were soft and unhurried, coming directly, unhesitatingly toward the door. Still crouching, holding the revolver in my right hand, I reached with my left for the light switch. Footsteps were just outside, I heard a toe strike against the threshold that had tripped me. Then they were in the room and I turned on the light.

I heard a breath drawn, just as the light switched on, but that was all. The yellowish light made everything reassuring and real; not eight feet away from me, covered by my revolver Mr. Moto was standing, motionless, but apparently not surprised.

Times such as those are glittering, jeweled instants which one can never forget. I remember exactly the way the light struck Mr. Moto's face, bringing out the eager, watchful lines around his narrow eyes, and making his blunt nose cast a sideward shadow on his coffee colored skin. I remember that he was smiling, with the curious reflex action of his race that makes the lips turn up at unconventional moments into a parody of merriment. Mr. Moto was the one who spoke first.

"Good evening," Mr. Moto said. "I am so glad to see you. What is the matter?"

When I answered him I was pleased with the steadiness of my own voice. There must have been a species of contagion in Mr. Moto's coolness.

"Moto," I said. "There is a chair just behind you, sit down." I paused and everything was growing very clear. "You eliminated Major Best with your crossbow, Moto, but you haven't killed me yet. Sit down, and I would not move if I were you."

Mr. Moto drew in his breath again and sat down quietly and folded his hands in his lap.

"Thank you," he said. "Thank you very much. I am afraid I do not understand."

I perched on the edge of my red lacquer desk and we sat for a moment looking at each other.

"That's exactly why I didn't shoot you when you came inside this door," I said. "I do not understand and you do not understand. I hope to find out what the trouble is before you go away. Three minutes ago a crossbow bolt went by my head. It's in the door frame now."

"Ah!" said Mr. Moto. "You were shot at? I am very, very sorry." He moved his hands slightly and I interrupted him.

"Quiet! Mr. Moto," I said. "Quiet, please."

"Yes," said Mr. Moto. "Certainly. I am so very, very sorry. You are right to be upset. I had no idea it would be so dangerous. I am very, very sorry."

We watched each other curiously. His eyes were bright but his face was expressionless. Then I spoke to him more sharply.

"You'll be a damned sight sorrier," I said, "if you don't explain right now. I'm not a fool, Moto. You killed Best last night because you thought that Best had told me of it. Speak up. What is it that you think I know? You tried to kill me in cold blood. I'll do the same to you if you don't speak up." I was growing angry as I spoke, and indignation was taking place of coolness. "You're a cold proposition, Mr. Moto, but I won't be a suicide to-night."

There was a flicker in Mr. Moto's glance. The gold work in his teeth glowed genially.

"Please, Mr. Nelson," he said. "Please. You must learn to take these things more calmly. I give you my word—"

"To hell with your word," I said.

"Please," said Mr. Moto, "I give you my word that I do not think you know anything. I came here out of interest in you, though I was very, very busy. Your gateman will tell you that I asked to come in. I did not try to kill you, Mr. Nelson."

"You didn't," I said, "but one of your men did, Moto. And furthermore — "

I actually found myself smiling. It is strange to say that such a moment was satisfying, but frankly it was so. I had never been in a position in my life before which had required definite, concrete action. I had something of the elation which comes of driving an automobile, or riding a horse and knowing that one is master. I was the master of Mr. Moto then; he was like a witness on the stand. I lowered my revolver an inch so that it covered the center of his slender well dressed torso, for someone had told me it was safer for a poor shot to try for the body and not the head.

There was no doubt that Mr. Moto was a cool customer. As far as I could tell from facial expression, he was enjoying the moment as much as I.

"My dear sir, you have the advantage of me to have studied the law," he said.

I kicked the desk with my heel.

"Exactly," I answered. "I know you went through all my papers. Why did you try to kill me, Moto? Who else are you going to try to kill? Miss Joyce?"

Mr. Moto half closed his eyes but those narrow, eager eyes of his never left mine for a moment.

"Please," he said. "My friend, I have had so many firearms pointed at me before that a man in my position is used to them. A servant of the Emperor is not afraid of death. It is a glory to him when he serves his Emperor."

"Don't talk rot," I told him. "I've heard a good deal about Japanese heroes. No one likes to die."

"You do not understand," Mr. Moto sighed. "Suppose I say I will not tell you anything? Suppose I ask you? What will you do then?"

I answered him coolly. "Killing in self defense is justified under the law," I said. "I haven't got many compunctions — not at present."

Mr. Moto sighed. "This is very unpleasant for me," he said. "Please believe me, I did not realize that this would happen. Think clearly, please, what it would involve should I have tried to murder you. I did not try. Instead a sensation of uneasiness crossed my mind about you, Mr. Nelson. Believe me, it was someone else who tried to kill you. Someone else, and I am very much afraid that he will try again. I am very much afraid — I began to be this morning — that Major Best was not a safe man to have seen last night."

"Who tried to kill me?" I asked. My mouth felt dry because I was close to believing him. "You'd better tell me, Moto."

"I am very, very sorry." Mr. Moto sighed again. "It will do no good to tell you, but I will tell you this because we are such good friends. Yesterday evening, your servant, who I do not think is a reliable man, had a letter addressed to you from America. I took the liberty to steal the envelope and to read it when I went through your other papers. I am very, very sorry. It was necessary to be quite sure of your position, since you were dining with Major Best. The letter contained a flattering offer for you to go home where you belong. Please believe me, you had better. If you agree, I shall see that you are safely conducted to the steamer at Shanghai. It would be very much nicer. I hope that you will go very, very much, please."

"Is that a threat?" I asked.

"No please." Mr. Moto seemed pained. "Please, I am your friend."

"Do you think you can ship me out of here?" I asked. "I've run my own business for quite a while, Moto, and I can run it still. You can't frighten me, Moto. I am staying. If you didn't try to kill me, who did?" I gave the revolver a jerk. "Out with it, Moto. We've talked long enough."

Then Mr. Moto did something which I have always admired.

"I am sorry," he said, "we have talked long enough." Still watching me, he rose deliberately and straightened the folds of his grey coat.

"Sit down," I said.

"Thank you," said Mr. Moto. "I cannot stay."

"Oh yes you can," I said. "Sit down."

Mr. Moto smiled at me brightly. "No," he said. "Thank you very much. I have done what I can for you, which is why I came. I've told you what I can. I have offered what I could. I am so sorry you are in danger. Very, very sorry. Please, you need not point that weapon at me, Mr. Nelson. I know that you will not use it because you understand that it will do no good. The consequences would be too grave for you. I am nothing. You are nothing. There are too many more like me to take my place. Besides, you are not the sort who kills. I warn you, Mr. Nelson, you are in a very dangerous position. You have been very stubborn. Now I must say Good-bye. I am so sorry."

"Did you hear me?" I said again. "Sit down."

He was calling my bluff and it made me angry. I could not have killed him if I had wanted, and he knew it.

"Good night," he said again.

"Oh no," I said. "Not quite yet." And I made a lunge at him, trying to grasp his shoulder, but Mr. Moto was very quick. His shoulder seemed to wriggle from beneath my hand, like an eel.

"I am so sorry," he said. "Good night!"

Before I could regain my balance and turn toward him, he was out the door and half way across the Court, and I was standing watching him go, not knowing exactly what to do. I had thought that I was master of the situation. Instead, I stood indecisively, with the revolver useless in my hand. Then I tossed the thing into my desk drawer. I was clearly not built for a gunman, and probably it was lucky that I put the gun away.

"You are in grave danger," Mr. Moto had said, and I believed it then. I even believed, in spite of my wishing not to, that someone else — not Mr. Moto — had tried to kill me.

I felt a keen awareness of danger for the next few minutes, a species of danger which was worse for being so entirely nebulous and unknown. Everything was a part of that danger. Everything which had happened. Best, the servants leaving, the questions of the picture dealer Pu, were all a part of it and beyond my powers of solution. They had all ended in the climax of the crossbow bolt, which was now in the frame of my door. Nevertheless, something was becoming definite. An idea came over me that made me cold inside. It was that man in coolie clothes, of whom Best had spoken. Best had been afraid of him. His name was Wu Lo Feng. If this man I had never seen had tried to kill me, it was because I had been with Best. Then I remembered that I was standing near the doorway with the light behind me. I turned and switched off the light.

These thoughts did not consume much time, not more than a few seconds, I suppose. I knew it was no time to sit thinking, and that thinking would do no good. There was a telephone on my desk and I reached for it in the dark, and called the number of the hotel where Eleanor Joyce was staying. In the interval, while I was waiting for her to answer, I became conscious for the first time that evening that I had been, and was still, afraid. When I heard her voice that fear left me. There was no mistaking her voice. It was cool and steady.

"This is Tom Nelson speaking," I said. "You recognize me, don't you? Are you all right?"

"Yes," she said, "of course." But then her voice grew sharper. "Why do you ask me that? Didn't I ask you not to call?"

It seemed wise to tell her then and there. I wanted her to realize that it was no laughing matter.

"Listen to me carefully, Eleanor Joyce," I said. "I am in my house. I have just been shot at with a crossbow. Does that mean anything to you?"

It did. I heard her give a low, choked cry, and then the wire was still.

"Are you listening, Eleanor Joyce?" I said.

"Yes," she said. "I'm listening."

"I'm afraid you're next on the list," I said. "Have you thought of that?"

Her voice was faint but it was steady. She was able to put two and two together.

"Yes," she answered. "I've thought of it."

"Wait!" I said. "I told you I'd come back if things got worse. Listen to me carefully. I am calling for a motor to take me to your hotel. Lock your door and don't let anyone in. Put down the shade and don't go near the window. Don't let anyone in until you hear me speak to you through the door."

There was a silence and then she said: "What are you going to do?"

"I'm going to take you to a place that is safe," I answered. "Now do exactly what I've told you. I'll be there as soon as I can manage."

CHAPTER XIII

I HUNG the receiver softly on the hook, at the same time barely restraining an impulse derived from past experience to call for a servant and to give directions to go out and fetch me a motor. The call was almost on my lips, when I stopped for two reasons. First, there were no servants except my loutish coolie who was sitting by the gate. I remembered that I had sent my ricksha boy to find someone to help with dinner, but this lack of service was not the only reason that kept me quiet. Some prescience of danger made me sit, mutely staring into the darkness of the room, nerves taut, irresolute. I felt safe there behind my desk in that room with its single open door, but the dark courtyard outside, which I would have to cross to reach my outer gate, was as heavy with danger as it was dark. A vivid imagination is not a pleasant companion at such a time as that, and I had never known that my imagination could be so vivid. I was peopling the courtyard with all the sinister, slinking figures of the Orient that adorn the pages of lurid fiction. All my confidence in my knowledge of

China left me for a quarter of an hour that night. While I sat behind that desk, my imagination was making me die a dozen forms of sudden death out there in the Court, but I knew I had to cross it to get away. I listened. I thought I heard voices, low, guarded voices from the servants' quarters by the gate, but there was no sound in the Court. I had sense enough to know that it did no good to wait. I picked up the telephone again, called a Chinese garage and ordered a closed car to be sent to my house at once. Five minutes later by my watch I tiptoed out the door into the yard, as nervously as though I were stepping into a tub of ice water. Nothing but a misplaced sense of pride prevented my bolting across the place to the pavilion which separated my inner Court from the outer garden and the gate.

Once I was around the edge of that grey brick screen designed to keep malign influences from my house, I sighed with pleased relief. The little paved Court by the red gate was alight from the windows of the kitchen and the servants' quarters. There were sounds of slippered footsteps and the clatter of dishes near the kitchen door and the smell of cooking. My ricksha boy had evidently found servants from among his friends or family. A sense of ease and comfort came back to me from the knowledge that my house was running again, miraculously if unsteadily, as houses run in China. Though I had ordered dinner and knew now that I would not be there to eat it, the knowledge that I was being served made everything secure. At the sound of my step on the brick pavement a man appeared in the doorway of the kitchen. I knew that he was one of the new servants though I could not see his face since his back was to the light — a tall, well built man dressed in the conventional long, white gown of service.

"The Master desires something?" he asked. He spoke in a dialect which was a little difficult for me to understand at once — one of the myriad local dialects which makes China its own great tower of Babel. His voice was smooth, rather high and bird-like, with a tinge of excited interest in it that did not go with the voice of a good servant.

"Are you the new man?" I asked him. "Where do you come from?"

"From the South City, if you please," he answered. "It was said you wished servants; I have brought them. I am the cousin of Yao, whom he promised when he left. I am only anxious to do what you wish, my Master." He walked toward me, bowing and his manners were not bad. "I hope I may give satisfaction," he was saying, "I understand foreign houses, I understand it is a great honor to serve the Master. I can manage as excellently as Yao."

"I shall not want dinner to-night," I said. I had no idea of mistrusting him and no hesitation at leaving this new staff alone in my house, for open theft is a rarity among the Peking servants, no matter from where they may appear. "I am going out now. I shall give you further orders and see if you are satisfactory to-morrow morning."

"What?" he said. It seemed to me his voice was sharper. "The Master is going out without his dinner? It is a very good dinner. It will be ready in an instant."

"I do not care to speak twice," I answered peevishly because I did not like his manner. "I said I am going out. Have the gate opened." I took a step toward the gate. To my surprise, the man moved in front of me.

"Master," he said again, "your dinner will be ready in an instant."

I did not answer. For a second I was too surprised to answer because the light from the kitchen door had struck his face. He stood in a frame of light against the dark, as perfectly as though the thing had been done upon the stage; his face appeared before my eyes as distinctly, suddenly and incontrovertibly. It was a thin, high, North China face, of a greyish brown, claylike texture. The nose was flat; the eyes were keen and slanting; the mouth was incongruous, a small budlike mouth of the Cupid's bow type. In that split second, before I could catch my breath, the words of Major Best came back to me. I could almost hear the Major's drawling voice:

"A little amusin' mouth, the sort you might call a rosebud mouth . . . a kissable mouth on a face like paste." I knew who the man was then. I was meeting, without an introduction, that erstwhile friend of Major Best, the bandit chief named Wu Lo Feng. It was Wu Lo Feng who was standing there, the new head servant in my house.

As I say, all this took an instant. There was no reason for him to think that I might recognize him but, of course, my face showed it. Now that Wu Lo Feng was in my house, I had a very good idea what he meant to do. Otherwise he would not have arranged to get there. The thought was like a dash of cold water. My surprise was so complete that I could not have moved in that second to save my life. I seemed to be temporarily detached from my own body, watching the whole scene from a distance. There was no doubt that Wu Lo Feng realized there was something wrong. There was no doubt that he was not going to let me out the door. I saw his eyes harden. His respectful look was gone and then he opened his rosebud mouth. I did not wait to hear the words that might come out of it. It was fear or some instinct of self preservation that moved me rather than any logic. I was close to him without knowing how I got there and my left fist and then my right were pounding on his jaw, in the one-two familiar to every boxer. I jumped away from him as he went down, crack, upon his hands and knees on the courtyard bricks. I did not wait to see what was going on behind me or if anyone had heard. Then I was snatching at the bar of the red house-gate; then I was out on the street. I heard the chatter of voices in the courtyard behind me but I did not wait to listen. The motor I had ordered was waiting by the door. I was inside it in a second.

"The hotel," I said. A shout from the half opened gate interrupted me.

"Has the Master forgotten something?" the driver asked. The engine was already going.

"No," I said. "Nothing. Hurry please because I am very late." And then the car lurched forward. I could see the driver's khaki clad back in front of me but I only half saw it. What I still saw, as though I had not moved away from it at all, was the face in the light of the courtyard, the face of Wu Lo Feng. The motor horn was blowing incessantly, a part of the technique of any Chinese chauffeur. I took out my handkerchief and wiped my face and then my hands, and I noticed that my hands were trembling.

That interlude seemed almost too grotesque to believe — that I should have been shot at, that I should have knocked a man down in my own courtyard, and should have made a dash for freedom out of my own gate. I was convinced by then that Mr. Moto was right when he said that he had not tried to kill me. I was caught up by something else and now I could not stop if I tried. I was in the midst of one of those upheavals about which I had tried to write. I was struggling against it but I wondered if my struggles mattered. Nevertheless, something mattered. For the first time in a long while I was not able to say to myself: "It doesn't matter, does it?" It mattered because I was instinctively sure that Eleanor Joyce was caught in the same current.

I told the car to wait when I got to the hotel. The lobby, with its tobacco stand, its desk, its glass cases full of curios, its tables where guests were drinking coffee, its clerks and its servants, seemed already like a part of another life, which I had left a long while back, a secure and easy life. I knocked on Eleanor Joyce's door and called to her. She opened it and I locked the door behind me. I was surprisingly glad to see her. She looked competent; much cooler than I looked, I am sure.

There was an unnatural sort of repression in that coolness which I did not like. She had been frightened when I spoke to her over the telephone, not twenty minutes before. Now she was controlled, and at the same time under some sort of nervous tension.

"I have some whiskey on the table for you," she said. "You had better sit down and take a little. You look as though it might do you good." Her tone made the picture wrong. I had come to help a damsel in distress and she was obviously trying to show me that help was not necessary. She sat down opposite me and raised her hand to smooth her brown hair. Her fingernails were shined to a high, meticulous polish which was like the veneer that had covered her the first time we had met. She was beautiful but entirely impersonal again.

"What are you looking at?" she asked. "Don't I look all right?"

"You look very well — too well," I said. "You had better put a dark coat over that white dress. We must leave here right away." But she seemed in no hurry to leave. Instead she lighted a cigarette.

"Now that you are here," she said, "tell me what has happened. Tell me slowly, please."

I told her, while she was smoking her cigarette. I told her of the shot and of the talk with Mr. Moto — concisely but completely; and I told her of my meeting with Wu Lo Feng. She listened as though we were complete strangers. When I finished, she smiled and nodded.

"You told that very nicely, Mr. Nelson," she said. "You have a gift for narration."

Then I lost my temper. It was her coolness that made me do so.

"Don't be ridiculous," I said. "I know you're mixed up in this thing. I'm not asking you how or why, but I've come to get you out of it. I'm not asking you who you are, or anything, but you'll have to do what I tell you now. You sent me away this morning; you can't send me away again. I want to help you. What are you laughing at?"

She was leaning back and laughing. It was one of the most exasperating moments I have ever known, to see her sit there laughing.

"Excuse me," she said. "I was just thinking of some of the things you said yesterday. You said you could show me the world but that I wouldn't care to see it. It seems to me I'm showing you something of the world myself, and that you don't like it very much. What was the word you used after we were dancing yesterday? Oh yes — it isn't very 'antiseptic' is it? You know so much of the world that you never get into difficulties, do you? I did think you'd be too careful to get yourself in such a spot, and too careful to be involved with a woman whom you don't know anything about. Don't worry, I'm not a bad sort of girl. I'm going to help you out. It was nice of you to come here. You have the proper instincts to help defenseless girls. You really are essentially nice, you know."

That speech of hers was so unexpected that I stayed quiet until I could control myself. I was angry and I did not wish her to see it because she might have laughed again. I am able to be sarcastic when I choose. I certainly tried to be when I answered:

"That's just what I wanted," I said. "I came, hoping that you might help me out. How do you propose to do it?"

"Easily," Eleanor Joyce answered. "When Americans get into trouble in China, kind friends send them home. Mr. Moto's suggestion is a very good one — that you go back to America and take up the loose threads of your own life. I shall take you to the American Vice-Consul's to-night, where nothing dangerous can happen to you, and you can take the Shanghai train to-morrow afternoon. That's perfectly simple, isn't it? Wait, don't interrupt me. As far as I'm concerned, I'm perfectly able to look after myself, and don't think I'm joking. When I tell certain people the mess you've got yourself into they'll make every effort to make you leave, don't you think? Perhaps I'd better get my coat, and we'll go to the Vice-Consul's now." She rose, and I rose also.

"That's a very good idea," I said. "I had never thought of going there for help. We'll go and we'll both go home together."

Eleanor Joyce shrugged her shoulders. "Oh no, we

123

won't!" she answered. "It's kind of you to ask me but I rather like it here. There are several things I have to do before I leave."

There was an ominous silence, which told me that I could not deal with her gently.

"Oh yes, you will," I said. "When I tell that Major Best was not a suicide. When I add that you were at his house and saw him die, I think you will go home."

Part of my speech was a shot in the dark, but it worked. I saw the color leave her cheeks.

"You wouldn't. You couldn't do that," she answered.

"I prefer not to," I said. "But I can and will, if it's going to leave you safe."

Then she changed. Her control left her so suddenly that I was startled. She bit her lip and her voice choked in a sob. "Don't you see?" she said. "Don't you see I'm trying to help you? I don't know why they're trying to kill you. If I can't make you, won't you *please* go away, for a little while at any rate? I was thinking of you, that's all."

"And I'm thinking of you," I said and I felt better now that I understood her. "You and I are caught in this thing, whether we like it or not. I don't know where you fit in the picture, and I don't believe you know yourself, but there's one thing certain. You can't go to any authority without getting into trouble. The same is true with me, in a lesser sense. At any rate I have no intention of going. So that's why you are going to do what I tell you."

She was cool again, and her voice was distant.

"Suppose I were to tell you," she suggested, "that I don't want your help, that I don't appreciate it, that I should prefer you to mind your own business?"

"It won't make any difference," I said.

"Why?" she asked.

"I don't know why," I told her, "but it won't."

"Suppose I were to tell you," she said, "that I am here for a reason that I consider very important and that your interference makes what I am doing very difficult. Would that make a difference?"

"No," I answered her. "None at all."

She turned away and sat down again. "Very well," she said. "I'm not going to leave this room."

There was not much doubt that she meant it. Her lips had closed in an unattractive, obstinate line. There was indication enough, if I had not guessed it before, that Eleanor Joyce was not an easy person to handle. I felt that I could sympathize with her relatives at home.

"You can suit yourself about that," I said. "If you don't go with me, I shall do just what I suggested. I shall call up someone in authority and he'll look after you. You can choose either way you please. It doesn't matter to me, as long as someone looks after you."

Her eyes snapped and her fingers clutched at the arms of her chair. I had an idea that she was going to spring out of the chair, and slap me.

"You can threaten," she said, "but you won't go telling tales. After all, you're a gentleman."

"After all," I repeated after her, "you trade on chivalry, in the end, like every other unattached woman, but this is one of the times it isn't going to work, Miss Joyce. I only want to see that you're out of harm's way. I don't think you have any conception what a mess you're in. You can choose, either me or the American authorities. You're choosing me? I thought you would."

She was out of her chair by then. "In case you don't know what I think of you," she said, "I may as well tell you. You're an incompetent. You're soft, and everyone knows you're soft. I'll be even with you for this. What ridiculous idea have you got that you can manage anything? Where do you think you're going to take me?"

I disregarded most of her remarks, though I did not like them.

"I'm going to take you where I think we'll both be safe," I told her. "I have a Chinese friend who will understand something about this, a rather good friend — Prince Tung. I'm going to take you to his house as soon as you put on your coat."

"You're going to take me to a Chinese house?" she asked. "You're not serious, are you?" Her voice was high and incredulous. "If you do, I'll find some way to pay you back."

"And I'll find out what you're doing here," I answered, "and why someone wants to kill me, and I'll probably save your neck. Here's your coat," I said, and I tossed it around her shoulders.

Eleanor Joyce snatched off her coat and tossed it over the back of the chair.

"There's no use doing that," I told her. "We're not going to wait any longer."

She hesitated. There was something else besides me that was troubling her. "I can't go yet," she said. "I'm expecting a caller and he'll be here any minute."

"You can leave word that you're out," I said. "The fewer people you see for a day or two the better."

I turned to pick up her coat again. As I did so, I saw something that interested me keenly. A Chinese painting scroll was lying on the table near one of the windows. I recognized the brocade on the back of it, a rich brocade of black and gold. I recognized the delicate work of ivory inlay on the wooden cylinder. It was the same picture, which had been in my house that morning.

CHAPTER XIV

"HELLO!" I said, "a scroll picture? I heard you were interested in art." I walked to the table to pick it up, but she was beside me before I reached it, snatching at my arm.

"Leave that alone," she said, "that's no affair of yours."

But I had the scroll in my hands already. "So you bought it," I said. "Pu came here with it, did he? That makes everything more interesting. I knew he never meant to sell it to me. I congratulate you, you must be rich, Miss Joyce."

"Put that down," she said. Her fingers tightened on my arm, her hands were trembling. There was something so insistent in her voice that I grew curious. Her agitation had made her unexpectedly appealing and she probably knew it.

"Please," she said, "please!" But I still held the picture.

"We'll take it with us," I said. "You don't mind that, do you?"

"No," she said, "we won't! It isn't yours, it's mine! If you don't put it down —"

There was a tap on the door before she could finish. "Stay where you are," she said. "I'll answer it." But I was at the door ahead of her.

I opened it a crack and looked into the hallway straight into the wrinkled and sparsely moustachioed face of the picture dealer, Mr. Pu.

His narrow, watery eyes blinked quickly, but he gave no other sign of surprise.

"Missy Joyce is here?" he said in halting English, looking directly past me.

I answered him in Chinese, a language which I knew Eleanor Joyce did not understand.

"The young virgin is going out," I said. "She has not time to speak to you."

"Missy Joyce," he said in a higher tone, "there is something I have to tell you."

Eleanor Joyce moved past me too quickly for me to stop her, pushed me aside and snatched open the door. Her color was high and her eyes were clouded with anger, but she favored Mr. Pu with a smile, which Mr. Pu returned.

"Come in, Mr. Pu," she said. "I've been waiting for you for a long while." Mr. Pu moved past me also in the centre of the room.

"Thank you, Missy Joyce," he was answering, "I am very glad you do not go out."

"So, that is what he was saying to you?" said Miss Joyce. She was furious. I believed in the next minute that she was not going to repress her anger but was going to make me the physical object of it. "So you were telling Mr. Pu in Chinese that I couldn't see him," she repeated. "Are you going to answer me? Were you or weren't you?"

"I was," I answered. I glanced at Mr. Pu meaningly. "And you are going to see as little of him as I can help. Mr. Pu came spying to my house to-day. He came with this same picture." I tapped the scroll beneath my arm. "But you didn't come to sell me that picture, did you, Mr. Pu? You came to find out what I was doing at Major Best's house last night and what Major Best told me. And now you're running around after Miss Joyce with this same picture. Are you trying to find out what Miss Joyce knows, Mr. Pu? And there is another question I want to ask you. What did you say about me to Mr. Wu Lo Feng that made him come to call at my house?"

I knew before I had finished that there was no use asking him these questions. I was only giving him a gratuitous advantage by showing that I suspected him. Mr. Pu's glance was of a bovine character. It was the glance of all his race, when it wishes to throw up black ignorance like cuttle fish, behind which it can conceal its thoughts. I was expert enough to see a little way behind that dullness and to know that my words were fast embedded in the mind of Mr. Pu. His contrition and his pain were too apparent. He was making too great a display of his venerable years. I had learned from past experience to be wary of Chinese merchants when they became voluble, venerable old gentlemen, and that was exactly what Mr. Pu had become, voluble, venerable, pained and ignorant.

"I no savvy what you say," he replied plaintively in broken English, obviously for the benefit of Miss Joyce. "I do nothing to you, nothing. No can help if Missy pay more for picture. All too bad."

I suspected that his volubility was dangerous, and that the less I talked to him the better.

"Come on," I said to Eleanor Joyce, "we're going."

"We're not going," said Eleanor Joyce, "until I've spoken to Mr. Pu."

"Remember what I told you," I warned her. "You can either come along with me or stay here. Just remember if you don't come with me I am going downstairs to telephone."

"There isn't any harm," said Eleanor Joyce. "I declare there isn't any harm."

But Mr. Pu was speaking already. His words were buzzing through the room like flies.

"Missy like picture? It's all same number one, like we say?"

"Yes," said Eleanor Joyce, "it's very nice."

"The others come all right to-morrow," said Mr. Pu. "You give me this now. You pay for all together."

"Yes, I said all," said Eleanor Joyce.

"And you give me this one now?" repeated Mr. Pu. He must have been greatly excited for he actually reached to take the scroll from under my arm. "You give to me, please," he said.

I pushed Mr. Pu away from me. "No," I said, "I'm keeping the picture. Missy is going out with me. We are going to show this picture to someone who knows about it."

No one who saw Mr. Pu's expression change as I did could speak any longer of the enigmatic Chinese race. I knew there was something wrong about the picture then. Mr. Pu was actually frightened, so frightened that he was trapped into saying something which I believed he did not intend.

"No, Missy," he said quickly, breathlessly. "Please, must not go with Mr. Nelson. You stay here. Here. All right. Everyone take good care. You go, all same very bad."

"It's going to be very bad for you if you don't get out of the way," I said. "Are you coming with me, Miss Joyce, or are you going to stay?"

"Oh, be quiet," Eleanor Joyce answered. "I told you I was coming."

She turned to Mr. Pu sweetly. "Mr. Pu," she explained, "I'm sorry to be so rude. Mr. Nelson wants me to see a Chinese friend of his who knows a great deal about pictures. I think I had better go. He says he will tell some things he knows if I don't."

Mr. Pu moved hastily aside. There was a watery light in his eyes as he looked at me that was not reassuring. Before Eleanor Joyce had spoken he had wished to have her stay and now apparently he wished to have her go. Once again Mr. Pu had found out something that he wanted.

"Yes," he said. "More better you go."

"But I'll see you later," said Eleanor Joyce, "won't I, Mr. Pu?"

I walked with her down the corridor to the elevator, pondering over Mr. Pu's behavior.

"You were very rude to Mr. Pu," said Eleanor Joyce.

"Well," I said. "It doesn't matter, does it? So he wants to sell you some more pictures, does he? Well, the quicker we get out of Mr. Pu's way the healthier it is going to be, I think."

"What makes you do this?" she asked me. "What possible reason have you got?"

"Lord knows," I answered. "I couldn't tell you." And I was right, I could not analyze my own motives. I could no longer tell, now that I had seen the picture and Mr. Pu, whether I liked her or disliked her. Whether she was dangerous, or a damsel in distress. I had thought that she was a nice girl, but now that she was dealing with Mr. Pu, I had an idea that she might be anything. I only knew that I was not going to be shot at again, if I could help it, because I knew Eleanor Joyce.

CHAPTER XV

I PRIDE myself that I know the city of Peking rather better than most Europeans, although no one can be wholly familiar with its infinite complexities, or can ever know all the secrets which lie between the blank grey walls of its narrow Hutungs.

There is too much enclosed behind the Peking walls for any mind, even that of an Oriental, which should know it best, to grasp. Its plan is too mystical, involved with the spirits of too many tortoises and dragons. There are the remains of too many dynasties, each imposed upon the other, shattered and warped like geological strata. There are too many temples, some living, some falling into ruin. There are too many public wells, and too many blind alleys. There are too many palaces, too many half-deserted gardens. The inaccurate hand of legend and mythology has covered the whole of it with glittering jewel-like tales of princes and princesses, of warriors and water carriers, till phantasy has mingled with geometrical accuracy, making the whole city as gloriously intricate as Chinese embroidery, where nothing is too small to be important.

I had spent a great deal of my time during my years in Peking in journeys through its streets in every quarter. I had seen enough of it to know that it would be a mystery, even after a lifetime. But I repeat, I knew it rather better than most foreigners.

It was nearly nine when I helped Eleanor Joyce into the automobile that was still waiting.

There was probably no reason to mistrust the driver, but I did not want him to know where we were going; also I wished to be sure that we were not followed. I prided myself that I could manage both those things. I leaned forward in my seat, and gave him a succession of orders, which must have made him dizzy. We went down the tramcar tracks to Tung Chang An Chieh, turned right on Hatamen Street and went through the gate in the wall of the Tartar City and past its towers and its outer bailey. Then we were threading our way through the complexities of the Chinese City and back to Chien Men, through the traffic by the railroad station. Once through the Chien Men Gate, we turned north up the Fu Yu Chieh keeping the waters of the artificial inland seas to our right, where the barges of forgotten emperors had plied once, through channels bordered by pink lotus.

The lights along the way were vague like the light from candles burning low. There is no place in the world as strange as Peking at night. When the darkness covers the city like a veil, and when incongruous and startling sights and sounds come to one out of that black. The gilded, carved façades of shops; the swinging candle lanterns; the figures by the tables in the smoky yellow light of tea houses; the sound of song; the twanging of stringed instruments; the warm, strange smell of soy bean oil; all come out of nowhere to touch one elusively and are gone. A life in which one can never be a part rolls past intimately but vainly. At such a time the shadows of old Peking stretch out their hands to touch you. You think instinctively of the days before the foreign domination, when Peking carts and man-born litters moved through the streets, with the lantern carriers walking ahead, bearing lights emblazoned with the master's name to light and clear the way. You think of the closed gates of the Forbidden City and of the watches by the City Gates. You think of the brass oil cups burning peacefully before the shrines of a thousand gods. You think of snarling temple lions and of the brooding, bearded figure of the God of War watching above the shadows of the Outer City Walls. The greatness and the peace of a better time comes back. You cannot get away from it once the night has fallen.

I looked through the back window of the car now and then, but nothing was following us, except the shadows of the street. We crossed Hsi An Men

Ta Chieh where one could catch a glimpse of the white dagoba beyond the Pei Hai bridge; then farther north, beyond Prince Ch'ieng's old palace, and farther still, where the tramway turns west toward the Hsi Chih Men Gate, I told the driver to stop.

"We'll get out here," I told Eleanor Joyce.

She had not spoken during all that ride. She did not speak then, until we were standing alone, on that dusty noisy street, beside the shop of a coffin maker who was still working with one of his assistants upon the latest of his wares.

"Where are we?" she asked. I did not blame her asking me because Peking is confusing at night.

"Don't worry," I said. "I know my way. We're going into the northwest quarter. It will be lonely, but it's perfectly safe." She did not answer, and we turned up a narrow unlighted alley, and stumbled in dusty ruts. As one examines the outlines of this corner of Peking, the maps have a mazelike complexity, reminiscent of puzzles so favored by psychologists to test the intelligence coefficient. The Hutungs, or alleys, open into irregular squares and taper off again into narrow meanderings. There are no street signs, and nearly the only light comes from occasional corner shrines, dedicated to the Goddess of Mercy, or to the Water God, or to the God of Earth. The walls of the hidden courtyards closed about us, making our footsteps echo hollowly. We turned corner after corner; we passed a coolie's eating house, and several dimly lighted food shops, but most of the quarter was asleep. Here and there were open holes dug for drainage during summer rains, which made our progress slow and awkward. Once I stumbled over a dog, sleeping in the dust, that yelped and snarled and ran away.

"Be careful," I said to Eleanor Joyce. "Walk close behind me."

It was very dark, and we were very far away from anything that was familiar. The age old sleep of China was closing over us, and we both must have been aware of our comparative unimportance, a disturbing fact for a Westerner to face.

"Are you sure you know where you're going?" she said at length. We had been walking for nearly a quarter of an hour by then.

"Yes," I said. "Wait a minute, we're nearly there." We stopped, and I listened, but the only sounds were peaceful sounds — the barking of a dog in the distance, quiet voices a long way off, and the faraway call of a ricksha puller, shouting for room. No one was following us; we went on and turned another corner, and there was a scent of fir trees about us, mingling with the age old stench of the alley. There were the fir trees of one of Prince Tung's gardens.

The wall to our left bounded an edge of the Prince's estate, in many respects a miniature of the Forbidden City, which had been laid out by the Prince's Manchu ancestors in the great days, centuries before, when the Manchus had come from the northern plateau to seize China by the throat, when their hands were strong, and their eyes were fierce, and their manners were uncouth. Though we were walking by the Prince's garden, it must have been eight minutes before we came to the Prince's gate. The iron-studded gate was forbiddingly shut, like the gate of a fortress. I groped for a rope, which I knew hung there, and pulled it hard. There was a clanging of a bell and silence. Then I pulled again and waited. The great days of the Tung family were over; there were no longer a dozen guardians at the gate; instead there was a shuffling sound of slippers on the pavement, and a grating opened, displaying an old man's face, who asked me who was there. I gave him my Chinese name and asked to see Prince Tung. He recognized me because I had been there often enough.

"The great master has gone to his sleep," he said.

I handed a five dollar bill through the grating, knowing that the servants of the Manchus were corruptible from the earliest days of the dynasty.

"Nevertheless, I must see him," I answered. "I am not here for nothing."

The money was as good as a key, as I knew it

would be. The old man drew the bars. The small door in the gate opened a crack, and he stood bowing, a slatternly old fellow in white coat and trousers holding a candle lantern.

"Will you please to come in," he said. "I will see that the great one is awakened."

Once we were in the courtyard, even the dim light of the old attendant's lantern sufficed to show that the greatness of the Tungs had gone the way of the dynasty they had supported, far on the road to ruin. The beams of the yellow light flickered against a dragon screen before the gate of writhing yellow and blue porcelain monsters, floating over clouds. There were gaps in the screen, where the tile work had fallen. Parts of the tiling still lay in fragments on the pavement. Behind the screen came one of those bare rock gardens so dear to the Chinese aesthetic sense, more grotesque in the yellow lantern light than it ever was by day. Jagged rocks were heaped up into artificial mountains, and into caves and gorges. We crossed a short foot bridge over a dry water course, and threaded our way through the rocks; we passed through a pavilion part of whose tiled roof had fallen, and whose latticed windows were broken and sagging. Then we were walking along the stone path, through a garden choked with weeds, past the ruins of summer houses and bridges, but the path itself was clear. It was one of those Chinese paths, designed with pebbles and cement in patterns of birds and flowers.

"Where are we?" said Eleanor Joyce, "where is this?" Something had made her voice hushed, and my own voice was low as I answered:

"We're in one of Prince Tung's gardens. There are acres of them, acres of ruined courts like this, and a theatre, and an artificial lake all ruined. The whole world of China was in here once. They always brought the world inside their walls. All the outside country was packed in here, the mountains and the deserts and the rivers. You see the Tungs were related to the Imperial family. He still keeps his gold-fish in the courtyard, here." We walked in silence through a moon gate in the wall to a low building in better repair than the others, which Prince Tung used for the reception of visitors.

The old man lighted a row of lanterns on the ceiling. As each new candle was lighted the long room grew more distinct. It was one of the most beautiful rooms that I have seen in any country. There was not a trace of Europe in that room. Pillars of camphor wood supported carved roof beams. The trim around the doors and windows was sandalwood, carved into a design of herons and lotus flowers. Poetry scrolls were hanging on the walls in bold black Chinese characters, the gifts of sages and emperors to the ancestors of the Tungs. Stiff backed chairs and tables of black and gold lacquer stood along the walls, the gift of the Emperor Chien Lung to the family. In spite of the years of neglect, the lacquer was as fresh and shiny as when the Son of Heaven had sent it there. The scrolls and the furniture were the only decoration in the room, but its austerity made it majestic. It was a place where pigtailed heads had pounded softly on the tiled floor when the master of the house appeared.

Once the lanterns were lighted the old man went away, and we sat each in a lacquer chair with a table between us. I said nothing, because the Prince's house always made me silent. I placed the picture scroll on the table, and looked at the shadows of the pillars that made black masses against the white paper windows. Eleanor Joyce was the first one to speak. She was interested; her resentment toward me seemed to have vanished.

"I'm grateful to you for taking me here," she said. "I didn't know there was a place in the world like this."

"There aren't many," I answered. "There aren't many foreigners who have seen this one, either."

A servant came through the open door, carrying a pot of tea and three cups. He set them on the table, poured us tea and left us. The taste of that lemon colored tea reminded me that I had not eaten dinner. We sipped our tea in a silence that was growing as stiff as the backs of the lacquer chairs. We must have sat there for ten minutes before Prince Tung came.

CHAPTER XVI

First there was a sound of slippers outside, and the rustle of a silk gown; then Prince Tung was standing in front of the table, in his black watered silk with his purple vest, and I had risen and was bowing. Though we knew each other very well, we went meticulously through the courtesies of the host and guest, because I knew that anything less would disturb him. We bowed and Prince Tung said: "I have not seen you for a long time." We had seen each other yesterday afternoon, but form was more important than fact.

"Has his Excellency been keeping well of late?" I asked.

I had enquired only yesterday afternoon for his health, but he thanked me floridly for my solicitude. I knew he was curious at this sudden intrusion, although he did not show it. We went through the formality gravely, like players through the opening of a chess game; and those formalities had a definite purpose, a realistic logic like everything else in China. They afforded a breathing space, in which each conversationalist might study the other, and form an estimate of the other's capacities, and decide what the other wanted. When I introduced Eleanor Joyce, Prince Tung accepted her presence suavely.

"He regrets that he cannot speak your language," I said to Eleanor Joyce. "He apologizes for his ignorance; he says your presence is an honor to his house."

Eleanor Joyce smiled icily.

"You can tell him it's lucky it is, if you want to," she said. "It isn't my fault I'm here. Does he mind if I smoke a cigarette?" She lighted one and gazed at us indifferently as we continued to talk, lost in her own thoughts; the bell like ripple of our conversation, with the four tones of the Mandarin dialect could mean less than nothing to her, which was probably just as well considering what the Prince said when the formalities were over.

"I do not understand," Prince Tung said. "I thought you told me the young woman was virtuous. How can she be virtuous if she is alone with you at night?"

"Your Excellency flatters me," I answered, "if he thinks every woman loses her virtue who is alone with me in darkness."

Prince Tung laughed heartily; he had an easy pliable sense of humor. "I have told you before, my dear esteemed friend," he said, "that I like you better than most of your round eyed countrymen. It is fortunate for you that you are growing too Chinese. It is not etiquette to ask why you are here. I sit in respectful patience until you speak."

I bowed to him, his manners always helped to make my own polished. "I am not worthy," I said. "Your Excellency is too gracious. I have come here to throw myself at your Excellency's feet, because my life was attempted this evening."

If Prince Tung was surprised he gave no indication; his hands with their tapering fingers rested conventionally and motionless, one on either knee.

"My chief dislike of foreigners," he said, "is their ungoverned temper. Rage is a disease."

"Excellency," I answered, "it was one of your own countrymen, not mine, who tried to kill me. I shall tell you about it if you are gracious enough to listen. Perhaps you may give me light."

"I declare to you," said Prince Tung, "that your account will give me the greatest pleasure, and that I shall endeavor in my dull way to give it my best attention." I could see that he did so, as I told him as accurately as I could, every word which had been exchanged with Major Best. He sat with his hands on his knees, his eyes unblinking, his sallow, rather rotund, face impassive, until I mentioned the name of Wu Lo Feng.

"That may indeed explain something," he said.

"Why the city is very restless for example, during these last few days. I told you there was trouble in the city, but I am wretchedly rude to interrupt. Your account, my dear younger brother, is too concise and charming to admit interruption, so very interesting. My people were clever with the bow, once. In my younger days I myself was obliged to shoot at a mark from a galloping horse, when the Bannermen gathered, at the Emperor's annual exercises. You know our interesting quarter, where the bowmakers still ply their trade? But my apologies, I interrupt."

He did not interrupt again, but there was a polite intensity, in the way he listened, that betrayed more than interest, almost agitation. I could feel it, for one's apprehension became sensitive after dealing with the Chinese. I could feel a growing excitement, although he sat there as impassively as a Manchu portrait. His eyes had never left mine, after I had mentioned the name of Wu Lo Feng. The lanterns glowed dimly in that Chinese room; my voice lost itself in the shadows of the rafters. I stole a glance at Eleanor Joyce; she was watching us incuriously.

"And so," said Prince Tung, after a moment's pause, when I had finished, "you are puzzled? There is nothing puzzling, believe me. It is only that the Middle Kingdom is in another of its periodic convulsions, such as occur inevitably after the fall of each dynasty. In a century or so, affairs will regulate themselves. There is little one can do during such interims. — So you brought the young woman with you? I speak to you as a friend, frankly and confidentially, because as I have said I have regard for you, though one's regard may be somewhat superficial beyond the family tie. You were not wise to bring this young woman, I think. One should be cautious in one's friendships, not swayed by passion or desire."

"Desire?" I said. "I have no desire."

Prince Tung smiled incredulously.

"A woman," he said, "is always dangerous, because eventually she is desirable."

"This one's not dangerous," I said. "One must protect women."

Prince Tung sighed. "That is one of the foreign concepts which I do not understand," he remarked. "It seems to me on the whole quite barbarous. Why should one protect women? Since when have they needed protection? Does this one need it? To me she possesses no attractive attributes."

Eleanor Joyce's voice interrupted us. Her instinct must have gathered that we were speaking of her. "What is he saying?" she asked.

"He's saying you're very beautiful," I answered.

"Oh," said Eleanor Joyce. Her hand went up to her hair, her fingernails glistened in the candlelight.

"You can see for yourself," said Prince Tung,

"that her gestures are crude and uncouth. She has been badly brought up by untutored parents. I repeat, I believe that she is dangerous."

"It is not so," I said. "It is because you do not understand my people."

Prince Tung paused and poured himself a cup of tea, took a sip from the fragile porcelain cup and set it down, unhurriedly. But I could see that something had disturbed him.

"I believe that I understand you better than you think," he said. "We Chinese are clever in gauging personalities. Just now you amuse me. Yes, I am very much amused."

"Why do I amuse you?" I asked. "I am so dull that I do not understand."

"You amuse me," Prince Tung's voice was gay and sprightly. There is an exasperation about the deflections of the Oriental mind; he seemed to have completely disregarded the seriousness of everything I told him. "You amuse me because we have conversed so often and so intelligently about the stream of history. We have agreed that no man can change events, and yet here you have been to-night, trying to change them. Though you admit it is futile, you have interested yourself in this young woman. It is always dangerous to interest oneself outside one's family, one is compelled there to make certain sacrifices, but never otherwise, never. Instead of allowing the course of events to shape itself, you have deliberately interfered."

He sipped at his tea again; then he drew a fan from behind his neckband, a gold and black fan like the lacquer of the chairs, and waved it slowly in front of him. I was obliged to admit that his words were true, that I was interfering instead of watching the world go by: yet there seemed no way out of it now that I had begun. Prince Tung snapped his fan together and replaced it behind his neck.

"You hope that I can explain these events?" he said. "I cannot very clearly. There is much that I do not understand. I do not understand how a picture should come into this affair. You have it here? May I see the picture?"

His black gown rustled softly as he rose, apparently taking permission for granted. He lifted the scroll from the table where the tea cups stood and moved with it to another bare table a small distance down the room, where the light from the painted glass lanterns was clearer. I watched Eleanor Joyce while he did so. Although she had been disturbed about the picture earlier, now she sat quietly watching Prince Tung. He was an interesting sight in the lantern light. The yellow gleam of candles picked out bits of a flower brocaded pattern in his black gown. His courtesy vest was a wine purple in the light, almost like the color in a stained glass window. He was leaning over the table, clearly in his element, a connoisseur examining an art object, as became a Manchu gentleman whose family had been distinguished patrons for generations. His fingers, delicate even for Chinese fingers, were unwinding the ribbon that held the scroll from around its carved ivory hasp. All his faculties were concentrating themselves upon the silk and paper before him.

"The brocade cover is not bad," he said softly. Then he was unrolling the picture deftly and I moved nearer and stood looking across his bent shoulders.

There is something theatrical in the construction of a scroll painting which reminds one of the pause in a theatre at home before the curtain is raised upon a stage set. The cylinder of paper which backs the silk is not only a protection, but a setting like a frame. The first part which is unrolled is exactly like the raising of a curtain; first nothing but blank paper appears between the hands, the mounting and the setting of the picture itself. You unroll the scroll for an appreciable time and see nothing but this blank space. There is a period of suspense and still blank silk or paper. Prince Tung's fingers moved swiftly while the scroll hissed comfortably beneath them, until the first of the picture appeared between his hands, flat on the table. The colors and the brushwork seemed to me truer and better than I had remembered. The beginning was a piece of Chinese mountain landscape, the tones of which might have seemed impossible if one had not seen the fantastic shapes of mountains in the clear yet dusky light of China; but once you had seen the Chinese country, the greens, the browns and the sapphires were no exaggeration, rather a part of an impressionism, delicate yet perfect and completely modern in conception, in spite of the centuries which divided its creator from the present. As I have said before, I had sense enough to know that the scroll was a piece of pictorial art of the very high order. Nevertheless I was not prepared for Prince Tung's reaction when he saw it.

At the sight of the first few inches of the painting, I saw Prince Tung's rather corpulent shoulders twitch. His fingers let the rolls go, so that they came together with a sudden swish. He straightened, and turned toward me so abruptly that I knew he was very much disturbed.

"What is wrong?" I asked. But already Prince Tung had partially recovered from his surprise.

"The picture is excellent," he said, although his voice was tuned to a new and elusive key. "I do not have to tell one who knows as well as you do that this comes from one of the finest periods. I am familiar with this particular picture. I have admired it twice in my life before. It is the work of the Sung Emperor and one of a set of eight, though it has been separate from the other seven for a long time. For three hundred years this single picture has been among the treasures of the monastery of Heavenly Benevolence in the Wu Tai Valley. Have you asked the young woman more about it? There is something which is not quite correct."

Prince Tung paused and pulled his fan from his neckband and flicked it open. I knew that it was a gesture designed to give him time for thought and also to supply a moment in which he might regain his composure; and his next words showed me I was right.

"I am afraid there is something very wrong," he said. "Something which I do not like. If this picture has appeared on the market here, the transaction is certainly irregular. I know the Abbot very well, my family has been accustomed to give presents to his institution. He valued this picture very highly. Now that it is on the market it can only mean one thing. The Monastery has been looted, the picture is a part of the loot, or else it has been stolen."

"What is he saying?" asked Eleanor Joyce. "Doesn't he like the picture?"

I walked across the room and stood near her. If the picture had been looted, I had a very good idea who had taken it and I wondered if she knew.

"I think you had better tell what you know," I told her. "Where did you hear about this picture?"

"What business is it of yours?" asked Eleanor

Joyce, but she moved uneasily in her lacquer chair.

"That's what I want to find out," I said. "I think you had better tell me, because if you don't I'll inquire of the police. The Nationalist Government is becoming interested in keeping such works of art in China. I can guess what you are doing now. I should have guessed before. Are you a museum buyer, Miss Joyce? Is that why you've been staying here for months? If you are you have done it rather well, although I don't like the profession. Are you going to tell me frankly or shall we have the whole thing public?"

She looked at me and hesitated. She was probably weighing possibilities carefully; but I knew that my guess was right before she answered. All sorts of past events were coming together to make it so, particularly what I knew of Major Best. Eleanor Joyce's glance did not waver, and when she answered her voice was matter-of-fact.

"The answer is 'Yes,'" she said. "You are right, Mr. Nelson. I was sent out here to buy a set of eight pictures. Word was sent to America that this set might be obtained. These pictures have often been mentioned by Chinese critics. They are listed in every history of Chinese art in fact, but they have not been seen for a long time. It is not our business how those pictures were to be obtained. I volunteered to come out and get them, pay for them, and bring them back.

I suppose you know that there are ways of managing these things. Well, this is one of the pictures. The other seven are to be delivered the day after to-morrow morning, and I say again it's not my affair where they may come from. I suppose most really great objects in China are acquired rather deviously and the more I see of this country the surer I am of it. Well, I was sent out here to get these pictures and I'm going to get them if I can."

Now that I understood what she was doing I thought she had done rather well, much as I disliked it.

"If you had told me that in the first place," I said, "everything would have been much easier. Who wrote to America and offered these pictures? Perhaps I can guess without your telling me — Major Jameson Best?"

"Yes," said Eleanor Joyce. "Of course he did."

"And you called at his house last night for the first picture? You did it rather well. Your people chose a good negotiator."

"Thanks," said Eleanor Joyce. "You're rather clever, Mr. Nelson. Yes, I called to get the picture."

"And you found the Major dead?"

Eleanor Joyce hesitated again, opened her lips, and closed them. Then she was looking at me as she had sometimes before, appealingly.

"I suppose I should have told you last night," she

answered, "but you see I was out here on confidential business. I was warned before I came that it might be shady but then there is always the argument, isn't there, that great works of art are safer in America? No, Major Best was not dead when I got there. I came, because he was to deliver to me the first picture last night. I was to examine it and pay for it. You may think I'm stupid but I'm rather good at pictures because I've studied them for years. Major Best was killed two minutes after I arrived, while we were standing in the doorway of his study. There was a snap, a twanging sound —"

"And then you ran away?" I said.

Eleanor Joyce nodded. "Yes," she said. "I ran away. You met me on the street, you were kind to me last night. I thought that was the end of it, and then the picture arrived late this morning after you came to call. I was warned to ask no questions, and I bought it. I repeat all this is my affair. I don't want you in it, I never have."

"I'm afraid it's late," I answered. "I'm afraid I would have been in it anyway." She did not answer and we looked at each other while the candles shone on the black and gold lacquer chairs. Perhaps we both were thinking how curious it was that we should have been thrown there together. Now that she had told me a part, everything that had happened was growing clear. If she had only told me earlier it might have saved us all this difficulty. At any rate, I could have told her a good deal about Major Best.

"I don't suppose you realize," she replied, "that all this means a good deal to me." I think she was glad that she was speaking to someone now that she had started. "I have always wanted to do something worth while and exciting. Well, I'm doing it and I'm going to see it through. You've seen that scroll. A set of such pictures are worth a good deal of sacrifice, aren't they? If I could see them somewhere safe I should feel that nearly anything was worth while."

"They should have sent a man out," I said. "None of these museum curators understand, or wish to appear to understand, how such purchases are made."

"Never mind," said Eleanor Joyce. "They probably think more highly of me at home than you do."

"No," I answered, "I think a good deal of your skill. What was the price asked for these pictures?"

Eleanor Joyce waited before she answered. "As long as I've told you this much," she said, "I may as well tell you the rest. The figure may raise your respect for me. The museum in America has offered twenty-five thousand dollars apiece for these paintings. The money is ready in the bank."

"Two hundred thousand dollars?" I asked.

"Yes," she answered. "Two hundred thousand American dollars. It is not a high price either." She mentioned the figure casually, but the price was high enough — high enough for bloodshed, high enough for anything, provided the proper people were involved. Certainly it was high enough for Major Best and Wu Lo Feng.

"Where are the other seven pictures coming from?" I asked.

Eleanor Joyce shook her head. "I've come across clean, as the police say at home," she answered. "I don't know where they're coming from and I thought it best not to ask. I was promised again to-day that they would be delivered the day after to-morrow morning at the latest. I think it was well enough not to ask, don't you?"

"There must be something else," I said, "that isn't all. Why should anyone want to kill me? It isn't my affair."

"I don't see why," said Eleanor Joyce. "That is something that I don't understand. Unless —" her glance grew suspicious, "unless there is something that you haven't told me. You're not buying pictures, by any chance?" The idea surprised me.

It surprised me so much that I grew indignant because of a perverse sort of sentimentality. Her suggestion placed me in that class of people who have preyed on a great country's weakness and cupidity. No matter what plausible reasons they might give they have never seemed a desirable class.

"No," I said. "You're mistaken. I'm not here to take anything away. I've asked nothing of this place except to be allowed to stay in it and to lead my life as I have wished. I have been allowed to, and I am grateful — too grateful to deal with picture thieves and grave robbers, or to make money out of misfortune. That sort of thing has never appealed to me."

I should have gone further because I was warming to my subject if Prince Tung had not interrupted me:

"It is a source of shame to me," he said, "that I have not been educated to learn your excellent language. It was considered barbarous and unnecessary when I was young, so that my teachers concentrated their efforts exclusively upon the great books of the classics, as it was intended that I should be a provincial magistrate. Yet I gather that the Young Virgin has been speaking to you freely. Would you be so gracious as to tell me because I am much interested in what she says about the picture?"

"She says it is one of a set of eight," I answered.

"Yes," said Prince Tung impatiently. "Yes, I know."

"And she says," I continued, though I could not gather how he knew that it was one of eight, "that she is buying all eight for a museum in America."

"What?" said Prince Tung. "All eight? I do not understand."

"I am only repeating to you what she has just

stated," I explained. "She says the other seven will be delivered to her to-morrow morning."

I stopped, astonished at the change in Prince Tung. For once he had lost his self control, his mouth dropped open, his fan dropped on the floor.

"Impossible!" he said. "It cannot be. No one has told me."

"How do you mean?" I asked him. "What disturbs you?"

Prince Tung stooped and picked up his fan, but his voice was still unsteady. "A great deal disturbs me," he answered. "I must collect my wits. I must try to think. The times are very unsettled. They are bad times in which to live."

"So you told me yesterday," I reminded him. "You said there was talk of trouble in the city, but what disturbs you now?"

Prince Tung looked around the room hastily, almost furtively. "My friend," he said, "I will tell you the truth. The matter which disturbs me is this. Those other seven pictures have been a treasure in my family for four centuries. They are in my possession now, in a strong room in this house."

"And you are going to sell them?" I asked him, because even then I could not understand his excitement.

"There is the trouble," said Prince Tung. "That is why I say the times are upset. It has not been suggested that I sell them. Nothing has been said about it whatsoever, and that means — " He stopped and fanned himself for a moment. "This is very terrible," he added. "Very terrible indeed. I had heard talk yesterday and to-day. I did not believe it. I considered it impossible."

"What?" I asked.

Prince Tung's forehead had grown moist. His placid eyes had opened wider but his manners were still impeccable. Nevertheless, he appeared to find it difficult to pay the proper attention to my questions. His mind seemed to have turned like a startled hare from actuality and to be running on a zigzag course of its own.

"I should have known — " he was saying vaguely, "I have recognized naturally that the man had certain capabilities even though he was the son of a Honan peasant, and in all probability illegitimate, yet I never conceived that he could be capable of this. I knew he was in the City but that there were any more along with him seemed to me incredible."

"Who?" I asked him again. "Who is in the City?" But the Prince did not answer my question.

"There have been instances," he said. "I recall some such similar event in the somewhat legendary period after the fall of the Chin dynasty. It is true that the army has been moved out of the City, but police have been watching the gates. I should have known that police are the same as soldiers, either ignorant or open to corruption. This is terrible. This is very terrible."

The excitement of Prince Tung was mounting as he spoke until he actually committed a rudeness. He turned his back to me and began pacing up and down the reception room. Once he actually forgot himself so far as to raise his arms in a futile, passionate gesture.

"Besides," he said, "I was definitely assured that I personally would not be molested. I was told that it would only be a small matter, only a slight disturbance. I should have known he would not stop at that. When a wolf is in the sheep fold — "

By this time I had lost my patience and I seized Prince Tung by the arm, although I knew that he hated to be touched.

"Who are you speaking of?" I asked. "Why don't you answer my question?"

Prince Tung wheeled around petulantly. "Why should I answer questions," he demanded in an exasperated voice, "if you have not wit enough to see? All foreigners are stupid. You are stupid. I am referring to Wu Lo Feng, of course, a bandit chief and an army leader. He is now in the city of Peking. He is here with several thousand followers who have entered disguised as peasants. Certain persons have been helping him for political reasons. Our local Governor is not popular with all parties, for instance. With the

Army gone there is an opportunity. Wu Lo Feng proposes to create a disturbance and to seize or loot a certain proportion of the City of Peking and now — ," Prince Tung slapped his fan against his palm, "and now he proposes to loot my property with the rest. It must be so, or why have my pictures been promised?"

"You are joking, of course," I said, but I knew he was not joking; whether the prospect was a possibility or not, it was real enough to Prince Tung.

It was so real that it shook him from his philosophic calm. His agitation was enough to prove that he believed it. Now that I thought of it, now that my mind was moving dazedly, the thing was a possibility. I could recall snatches of my conversation with Major Best and when I did so, I knew that he had believed it. There must have been a rumor of it, running as rumors do in China in strange, backwater channels. Mr. Moto must have heard that rumor. It accounted for his sudden interest in what had been said last night. It accounted, in a way, for what had happened to me this very evening. There was not much time to think because Prince Tung's voice was rising higher.

"I was a fool," the Prince was saying. "Why did I not bring my pictures and my porcelains to the bank this morning! Now, I must do something, I must try to think."

"If you're serious," I told him, "there's always the police." Prince Tung laughed mockingly.

"I should have thought," he said, "that you might have learned enough of our institutions to understand that officials are always difficult. One can never tell in these days in what direction an official may be involved and I have not time to consider whom safely to approach. I must act at once, at once." The idea of the Prince acting was suddenly amusing, in the light of what he had said a few minutes before.

"The Great One is inconsistent," I said, because even then the idea of anyone seizing Peking seemed too fantastic to be possible. "The Master is not moving with events, he is trying to interfere with them. Surely, you recall how often you have said these forces cannot be stopped."

"Don't be a fool," said Prince Tung sharply. "This is not a time for philosophy. So you don't believe me? Well, perhaps you will believe me when we are dead to-morrow morning and the streets are running blood. Something must be done at once. We must get to the hotel in the Legation Quarter, we must get — "

An exclamation from Eleanor Joyce interrupted him.

"Tom!" she called sharply, "there are people outside. The place is full of people."

The Prince and I must have been very much absorbed in each other. At any rate, I had noticed nothing until Eleanor Joyce spoke. There were two doors to the Prince's reception pavilion, each nearly opposite to the other. Prince Tung and I were standing between these doors, in the centre of the room. As I looked around when Eleanor Joyce spoke, I saw that there were men in either doorway and that they were not members of the Prince's meagre staff of servants. They were dressed in that characteristic blue cloth of China. They were large-boned, competent men, not of the city type. Their faces were dull and heavy in the lantern light. They were crowding in through the doors, cautiously but efficiently. In that instant, before I could think who they were or what to do, I could smell the garlic on their breaths and I could hear their heavy breathing. Prince Tung must have seen them at the same moment and his reaction was admirably in keeping with the training of a Manchu gentleman.

Prince Tung flicked open his fan. "It is too late," he said, "Wu Lo Feng's people have come. I am very much afraid this is the end."

I was inclined to agree with him, without knowing the correct reason for it, that he and I were close to the end of our careers. The faces of our unexpected visitors indicated this prospect rather clearly; they were in a circle about us by that time. The air was nauseating from the garlic, to me at any rate, although I suppose that Prince Tung had that obliviousness to unpleasant odors which is one of the virtues of his race. I had seen similar faces before, though never as intimately. I had seen the same stamp on the features of disbanded soldiers and on bandits caught by the authorities and waiting to be shot. Our callers all possessed a cast of countenance peculiar to distracted times anywhere in the world. And yet I liked them, perhaps because I have always found the Chinese in nearly any circumstance the most agreeable people in the world. I could not help but feeling that, given a change of mood, nearly all of these men would be as courteous and agreeable as the crowds I had known before. Their expression on the whole was more bewildered than brutal — the puzzled expression of individuals forced by fortune into a situation for which they were not particularly fitted. They were forced by fortune to be desperadoes, but they still had the courtesy and the patience of their race. I repeat even at that moment I felt kindly disposed toward them. Somehow I could not take them entirely seriously.

I noticed in that brief moment that every one of these fellows, in spite of their coolie rags and torn slippers and bare feet, was armed quite efficiently with Webb belts and revolvers. I remember thinking while I gazed at them that their weapons were out of place since those men did not belong to the enlightened present. Rather, we seemed to have been sent back into some fabulous time of the Middle Ages as soon as they appeared. I remember thinking that China is probably always like that, once one penetrates beneath its surface efforts to be modern. There is always the venerable past, the immense accumulation of consistent and interrupted experience, which makes modernism as we know it quite impossible.

In the midst of these vague impressions was a more definite, immediate thought. No matter who the people were who surrounded us, they were killers. It was only a question whether it was convenient to eliminate us then or later, and Prince Tung must have shared in my opinion. I saw his eyes move dully from face to face, incuriously, not expecting hope or mercy, while he waved his fan in front of him because the room was growing stifling hot. It became apparent to me that I was looking on a scene which had repeated itself almost endlessly in the cycles of the Middle Kingdom. The last of a weary, conquering race was waiting to be eliminated by a new conqueror, as an inevitable part of evolution, expecting nothing else, just as the Manchus expected nothing less than universal slaughter when the Allies in the Boxer days stormed and took Peking.

Prince Tung asked no foolish question. He had already singled out the leader, a pockmarked northern peasant with the skin and yellowing eyes of the confirmed and heavy opium smoker. Prince Tung did not ask how the men had appeared so noiselessly, whether through skill or treachery; he expressed no indignation or surprise; he simply gazed at the pockmarked man.

"What is your desire?" he asked. To the pockmarked man the inquiry appeared to be equable and natural. He slapped his right hand noisily on his pistol butt, for a Chinese is nearly always fond of noise and theatre. He opened his mouth and answered in a crude dialect, between decaying stumps of teeth.

"The Commander Wu Lo Feng will see you and this foreigner and the woman — or we will kill you now if you do not wish to see him."

The proposal was eminently simple. What surprised me most was that I felt no fear but only amazement that I should be taking part in such a spectacle. Perhaps the reason was that physical fear seems to dwindle to a negligible emotion in such a country, where human life is not of very great importance. I was living abruptly in an environment which others had told about but which I have never expected to see, and probably I was more stunned then by the unreality and too curious to be afraid. Prince Tung made his decision immediately, though not with joy.

"We will go," he said and put his fan behind his neck and cast a melancholy, sideward glance at me.

"I suppose I shall be tortured," he added. "This is very bitter."

It was obvious enough that Eleanor Joyce and I were also expected to attend on Mr. Wu Lo Feng. Although we had not been followed, as far as I had been able to ascertain, we had been traced in some way. I had an impersonal sort of curiosity as to how this had been done, but it was as vague as my other emotions, until an event occurred which answered both the lingering questions and gave me a sickening sense of reality.

Just as Prince Tung finished speaking there was commotion at one of the doorways. Someone was pushing his way through the crowd. I followed the movement indifferently until I saw who it was. It was the curio dealer, Mr. Pu. He bowed to me, without any animosity.

"I see I am right," he said. "When you told me you were going to show the picture I judged it would be here. Now I will take it, if you are quite finished."

"Take it as quickly as you can," I said. His presence gave me a sort of hope. I was pleased at any rate to see a familiar face which had some connection with the tranquil days I had known. "Take it, Mr. Pu, and get us out of here. I will make it worth your while. Miss Joyce and I have nothing to do with this. Tell these men, whoever they are, it is dangerous to meddle with foreigners."

Mr. Pu's eyes were watery, but alert; I shall always remember him as being very business-like that evening and I shall remember that Chinese curio dealers, even those of an advanced age, may be men of great capability.

"I am sorry," said Mr. Pu. "It is too late now, I think. Please do not be so stupid as to make resistance. These men are very rude." He turned away from me to speak to the leader.

"The young woman is to be treated gently. Put a handkerchief over her eyes and lead her to the automobile. The men will be tied and gagged."

Then he spoke to Eleanor Joyce in his pidgin English:

"All right, Missy," he said. "You go along with these men, please. It will be all right." Two men had taken her by the arms, a third was tying a white bandage over her eyes.

"Go ahead," I said to her. "Don't be frightened, we'll be with you."

My advice did not imply any great reassurance but it was the only thing that I could say. When they led her out of the room she did not speak but walked quietly. I was thankful she was gone, a second later.

"Very well," said Mr. Pu, "now you may arrange about the others."

The leader was about to give an order when someone in back of the room asked a question.

"What about the old man?" a voice asked. "The gate man, shall we bring him too?" The leader made a curt, angry gesture.

"No, you fools. Where is he?"

"Here!" said someone. There was another disturbance at the outside of the circle around us and an old man in a white pyjama suit, with his hands tied beside him, was pushed into the centre of the circle. He stumbled and fell on his knees not a yard from where I was standing. Someone in the crowd laughed. There is not much pity for human misery in China. I recognized him as the old man who had let us in through Prince Tung's gate.

"He may make trouble if you do not take him," said Mr. Pu.

"Well," the leader said, "kill him then. What are you gaping at? Kill him I said . . . someone with a sword. And tie the arms of this foreign barbarian."

What happened next was so quick that I could not believe it. The men were evidently efficient and accustomed to their work. Two of them had seized hold of me, heavy sweaty fellows, with torsos like wrestlers. My hands were snapped behind me, a rope bit into my wrist. I hardly noticed it, however, because of my sickening concentration on the scene in front of me. The old man still knelt, with his hands tied beside him. He made no plea for mercy. He was obeying some unwritten rule of Oriental etiquette — facing the inevitable with the stolid, desperate fortitude of the Chinese peasant, who knows when his time has come. He appeared to share with all his countrymen the idea that his death was logical. Certainly no one in the room thought otherwise. A fellow in blue dungarees had stepped behind him, holding one of those huge, machete-like swords that one still sees slung across the backs of Chinese soldiers.

"Bend your head," he said. And the old man bent his head. I was afflicted with a momentary nausea and dizziness. I had an instinct to cry out. Perhaps I did, but I cannot remember because the thing was over in a moment. The man with the sword made a grunting sound, like a chopper in the woods and the old man's body lay, headless, on the floor.

"Quickly!" I heard the leader say, "quickly!" And that shocking sight was blotted out. My eyes were blinded and a filthy rag was stuffed into my mouth. I only knew that I had had a glimpse of China which had been kept from me until then, a glimpse of the supreme, callous, mercilessness of that land of over-abundant life.

CHAPTER XVII

I WAS tied up like one of the black, Chinese hogs
for its trip to the market. I must have struggled in-
voluntarily when another rope bit into my elbows,
for someone hit me a heavy blow on the side of the
head that sent my senses reeling. Everything was
black and all my impressions became vague, what
with the blindfold and the gag and the blow on the
head.

The whole business must have been carefully
planned by individuals who were specialists in the
art of kidnapping and ransom. We were being carried through the courtyards, and next we were
thrown into an automobile. Even in the best of times
a lower class Chinese does not give much thought to
personal comfort, and we were not being treated
with particular consideration. I was doubled up, half
on the floor and half on the seat, with my legs and
arms growing numb and my back strained and ach-
ing. We were being taken somewhere but it was not
for me to reason why. Nevertheless, I must have done
a good deal of thinking on that ride, mostly on the
subject of how suddenly life can change. Details of

the tea party of the day before moved across my consciousness, in an irrational, half delirious chain. I could almost hear the cool clink of cocktail glasses. I could see the dancers on the terrace . . . Eleanor Joyce in her green dress dancing with the Attaché from the Italian Legation . . . the champagne corks were popping in the dining room of Major Best.

"He simply sets a straw beneath his subject's epidermis," Major Best was saying, "then everybody interested takes a blow on the straw. I saw Wu do it myself in the mountains outside of Kalgan. . . . I'd put him above the old Marshal of Manchuria for brains . . . they made the Chinese Army move out of Peking . . . anyone could take Peking. You and I could take it if we had a couple of thousand men."

Everything was impossible. It was impossible that I was there. What I had seen and heard were all impossibilities. Yet there I was in spite of them, caught in one of those erratic tides of the distracted country which I had thought I loved; and I still loved it in a way. There was no use in struggling against the tide, but still I had a distinct desire to struggle. It surprised me to realize that the desire was not wholly one of self preservation. Pride had something to do with it, and there was more than that. Eleanor Joyce was with us, a picture buyer for an American museum, engaged in a manipulation of which I could not approve. I was quite sure by then I disliked her. Nevertheless, we were of the same race; she had said the other night that we were the same sort of person, and perhaps we were. If there was anything that I could do to get her safely out from where we might be going, I knew almost against my will that I should be obliged to try.

If you have ever travelled by railroad around the outer walls of Peking you have an involuntary respect for the city's area. We were carried by motor and the journey fortunately was not as long, but it was long enough. At the end of twenty minutes or perhaps half an hour, the car stopped and I could hear the creaking of large gates being moved; then the car crawled forward in low gear into what I judged accurately was a large courtyard where it stopped again. I was lifted out, still like a market pig, and as my ears were not closed I heard a number of low-voiced remarks about my personal appearance while I was being carried *somewhere,* to judge from the smell and the coolness, into a large and little used building, where my bearers stopped and tossed me on the floor.

Then a voice said: "You can untie them now."

The cords were removed from my arms and legs, but even so I was too numb to move. A minute later I did manage, however, to pull myself into a sitting position and to wrench the rag out of my mouth and the bandage from my eyes. It was somewhat like the return of consciousness once my sight was back. My first sensation, before my mind registered any impression, was one of acute bodily misery.

My tongue and mouth were distorted and swollen from the cloth that had gagged me; my arms and legs ached from the effort of returning circulation. The first thing I did was to cough and spit and try to rub my wrists and ankles; then I got on my knees and pushed myself to my feet.

There was a kerosene lantern beside a doorway where two men armed with rifles were standing, evidently a guard. Although the light was dim enough, it was sufficient to show the nature of the place. I was evidently in one of the buildings of an abandoned temple, one of the scores which are tucked away in corners of the city, now almost nameless and forgotten in that place where there is little respect, in spite of ancestor worship, for the works of past generations. Like so many of these buildings, the only light came from the doorways which now were closed and through windows which were boarded up. Thus the room, even with the lantern in it, was sepulchral and solemn; its corners were a mass of shadows which seemed to be moving visibly against the ring of light. This sense of light and shadow gave every visible object a scale that was grotesque and disproportionate. Columns of camphorwood rose up into the pitch blackness of the roof, like the stalactites of a cave; dim, faded frescoes of Buddhistic disciples made dreamlike patterns on crumbling plaster walls. It was a long while since incense had been burned to the gods. The figures on the central altar had nearly all been removed or destroyed, but various disciples easily twelve feet high stood on pedestals in front of the frescoed wall, their gilt paint cracked and tarnished, half distinguishable, mouldering works of mud. They stood there as inarticulate and as problematical as fate. A Chinese temple in disrepair is always an eerie place; a monument more to futility and cynicism than to the involved mysticisms of the Buddhistic faith.

I was standing in the space before the central altar. After those first dazed seconds of instinctive adjustment to my surroundings I saw that I did not have the apartment to myself. Prince Tung was standing near me, brushing the dust from his black silk robes, and Eleanor Joyce was helping him. I walked toward her rather unsteadily and asked her how she was.

"Thank you," she said to me formally. It is odd what people say in such circumstances. "I can manage. I'm quite all right."

"That's very nice," I said. "I'm very glad to hear it. An interesting spot, isn't it? Since you are an authority on art, where would you place these frescoes? Probably rather late Ming would you say? But restored in the seventeen hundreds?"

Her blank stare made me aware that my speech was peculiar under the circumstances. As a matter of fact, my mood was as peculiar as my speech. I was angry at the treatment I had received, but it was a stimulating sort of anger. It had whipped my spirits into a perverted sort of gayety. It had stimulated me for the time being, beyond any great sense of pain or discomfort.

"You're hurt," said Eleanor Joyce. "Did they hit you?"

"Just an affectionate slap," I answered. "Probably nothing to what's coming." And then I lowered my voice. "Don't be frightened," I said. "Don't let them see you're frightened. Everything around here is a matter of face."

"Yes," she answered. "Yes, I understand."

"You only have to look at Prince Tung," I suggested, "don't make him ashamed of us."

"No," she said, "I won't."

I was proud that I knew Prince Tung. If ever there was an example of inbred self control, Prince Tung was its perfection. The Prince had dusted himself off carefully and now he was looking about him with scholarly curiosity, as though he had been set down purposely, on a tour of pleasure.

"It seems odd to me that I have never been in this temple before," he said, "but then there are so many interesting monuments to be visited that only an antiquarian could be supposed to have the time. Evidently this has had some bad luck connected with it, just as we have had bad luck now." He looked coldly at Eleanor Joyce. "To have the female element of creation, the Yin, connected with affairs, frequently presages bitterness and misfortune. No, I have never been here, though I have some recollection of this place being mentioned in the old days of the Court, and I have a suspicion that we are near the East Straight Gate which was provided with a bell instead of a gong. There is an amusing story about it that doubtless you have heard."

"No," I said, "but if you should condescend to tell the story, what would be more fitting, considering the time and place?"

Prince Tung sighed.

"I am growing old," he said, "and somewhat unused to rough handling, but polite conversation removes the mind from the immediate. I must say for you, my friend, that you are conducting yourself up to the present in a far better way than most foreigners. You have not lost your temper. You are neither blaspheming or giving way to useless activity or useless speculation. Yes, the story is amusing, and it may promote tranquillity to tell it. I am sorry that the young virgin cannot understand me, but it may be that there will be ample time for you to translate my remarks." Prince Tung rubbed his hands together, and I actually found myself half-listening to his story.

"It appears," he said, "during some period in an earlier dynasty, that a young Bachelor of Arts was approaching this gate of the city in order to take the metropolitan examination. As he neared the walls he encountered a tortoise, disguised as a scholar."

"A difficult disguise," I said.

"What is he saying?" Eleanor Joyce asked suddenly, "aren't you going to do anything? Where are we? What has happened? What is he talking about?"

"About a scholar disguised as a tortoise," I said.

"Dear God!" said Eleanor. "Are you both going mad? Aren't you going to do anything?" I took her hand and drew her near to me.

"Don't interrupt," I said. "Prince Tung knows more about this than you or I. Prince Tung is always correct. There is nothing possible to do except to wait just now."

"A difficult matter of disguise, as you say," Prince Tung said placidly, "but at the same time possible. Both the Bachelor of Arts and the tortoise stopped at an inn outside this gate. 'It will be your fortune to see the Emperor,' the tortoise said, 'because you will take a first degree in your examination. When you see the Emperor will you do me a favor? Will you please to ask him when I may come into the city and go up for my examination?' Matters came to pass exactly as the tortoise had predicted. The scholar took

181

a first degree, and when he came back to the gate again he stopped to see the tortoise. You understand that he had the interests of the city at heart?"

"Yes," I said, "naturally I understand." I said it, but as I listened to the folk tale I could almost agree with Eleanor Joyce that we were both a little mad, although the madness seemed quite natural.

"And the scholar said to the tortoise," continued Prince Tung, " 'The Emperor sent you this message. When the gong on the East Straight Gate is struck it will indicate that you are summoned for your examination.' You understand the significance of this, of course? It is hardly necessary to add that the scholar in all haste repaired to the suitable officials. The gong on the East Straight Gate was removed and the bell was set up in its place. Thus the tortoise is still waiting outside the gate, and thus he has not been offended. You understand how important all this was."

In spite of myself my mind was wandering. There were sounds outside the temple door of footsteps and voices. "What did you say?" I asked absentmindedly. "Perhaps I don't understand after all, I'm sorry." Prince Tung surely must have heard the voices too but he gave no sign of interest. He smiled at me mockingly and rubbed his hands together.

"I regret that I have outstripped your great knowledge of our country," he said. "I had taken it for granted that you would be completely acquainted with our symbolism. The tortoise is the sign of floods; thus one could naturally not let him into the city, and at the same time one could not offend him. And now my story is over at exactly the right moment. See? The main temple door is opening."

The two guards by the door straightened and had put their rifles at a rough imitation of European port arms. I do not know what I expected to see come through the door but certainly not what I saw. Three men entered carrying a fourth, bound and gagged, just as we had been. They tossed him on the floor, untied his ropes, turned and walked out.

"They've brought someone else," said Eleanor Joyce. It was an idiotic remark but I did not tell her so. I was gazing at the figure on the mud floor. It was a small man, in a light gray business suit which was torn in several places and spattered with mud. For a moment I could not see his face because a bandage was still across his eyes. His head was bleeding from a scalp wound and he was lying motionless. The guards by the door stared at him placidly. They made no objection when I walked over to him. I put my hand beneath his head and pulled the gag from his mouth. The man was a Japanese but even before I took the bandage from his eyes I knew who he was and so did Eleanor Joyce.

"It's Mr. Moto!" she said.

CHAPTER XVIII

"Moto," I was saying, "do you hear me, Moto?"
It was Mr. Moto sure enough.

I got my arm beneath his shoulders and sat him up.
It was easy enough because he must have weighed
less than a hundred pounds. I took my handkerchief
and wiped the blood from the scalp wound on his
head. As I did so, Mr. Moto opened his eyes and drew
in his breath with a sharp, conventional hiss. He
recognized me at once, and Mr. Moto had his manners too, as good in their way as Prince Tung's. His
dark eyes flickered.

"Thank you," he said, "thank you so very much.
I am sorry to have troubled you, sorry to have spoiled
your handkerchief. Good evening, Mr. Nelson. I am
so sorry to see you here, very, very sorry. Will you
help me to my feet, please? Thank you, now I am
quite recovered."

"Are you recovered enough," I asked, "to tell us
what we are here for?"

If Mr. Moto was in pain his expression did not

show it. The gold fillings of his teeth glittered in a mechanical smile and he pressed my handkerchief softly to the side of his head.

"Certainly," said Mr. Moto, "I can tell you. It was what I suspected, but now I am quite sure. Thank you for the handkerchief, so very, very much. Sometime, Mr. Nelson, I hope very, very much that I may buy you another, please. Yes, I shall tell you why we are here. I think, I am almost sure, that a man named Wu Lo Feng believes that we all know that he is proposing an outlaw military demonstration in Peking. Being afraid we might tell of it he brought us here. He killed Major Best for the same reason. Why he did not kill the rest of us I cannot quite imagine. I have no doubt we shall know however very, very soon."

When Mr. Moto with sharp, staccato words ceased, Prince Tung did a surprising thing, yet not so surprising if one is familiar with the Chinese point of view. The Prince walked toward the door and spoke to one of the guards.

"We have not had tea," he said. "We are fatigued, we desire some tea."

The guard stared at him stupidly, then he opened the door a crack and bawled into the dark outside:

"Tea," he said, "the prisoners desire tea." And strange as it may seem, a man appeared a minute later with a pot of tea and four cups.

"That is much better," said Prince Tung. "Now we shall be more comfortable, I think."

Prince Tung placed the blue wire-handled teapot upon the dusty altar. He looked like a temple attendant as he poured out four cups of tea. He glanced at Mr. Moto with placid and resigned recognition. "You have the advantage of me," he said, "in being able to speak the excellent though rather limited language of the West. No doubt you were explaining something to our excellent friend Mr. Nelson. Could it be that you might be gracious enough to repeat it to me, in my own poor language, simply to satisfy my own curiosity, not that it will do much good? This tea is wretched, but at least it is quite warm." Mr. Moto mopped at his head again.

"His Excellency has been an enemy of ours for a long while," he said in Mandarin, "but I shall be glad to tell him." I handed Eleanor Joyce a cup of tea while he was speaking. She had evidently understood the significance of Mr. Moto's explanation, short though it had been. I tried to say something calm and cheerful.

"It looks as though we were caught up in a little war," I said. "Such things have happened in outlying provinces but I never expected to see anything like it here. We always think that nothing will happen." She looked frightened and I did not want her to be afraid.

186

"Do you really mean that bandits have got into Peking?" she asked.

"It looks that way," I said. "That's what comes of buying casual works of art. That's why you are here to-night."

The color came back to her cheeks. "Well," she said, "it's a chance I took. I guess I can stand it if you can. You are calm enough about it. Are you always so calm about everything?"

I shrugged my shoulders and drank my tea. As a matter of fact I was far from feeling calm. The significance of what was happening was a good deal clearer to me than it was to her, and there was no use disturbing her with the significance. Mr. Moto had thrown nearly the last ray of light upon complications which were now becoming simple. My legal training had shown me before that the most involved human combinations grow geometrically plain once the motives are revealed. This gradual elucidation was absorbing enough to make me half forgetful of where I was, now that the cards were falling on the table. The figure of a single man whom I had only seen for a moment stood in the shadows behind those motives; the half-mythical, dreamlike figure appealing strongly to any height of the imagination; the man with the rosebud mouth, the kissable mouth; the bandit chief named Wu Lo Feng. He was not there but he was somewhere just outside, almost the last of the unknown quantities. Just now he held all of us in the hollow of his undoubtedly grimy hand, a clever man, an able man, as Major Best had said. Each moment I experienced a growing respect for the abilities and the motives of Mr. Wu Lo Feng. I had respect enough to realize that I was perspiring clammily. He had killed Major Best because the Major, through some past acquaintance, knew what he was doing. He had tried to kill me because he had thought that the Major had told me the secret. Now he had caught all four of us because he thought that we all knew it. If the secret involved an uprising inside the city, I did not blame him for his caution.

We were all there for different reasons, each because of his own motives. Mr. Moto and Prince Tung were glancing at each other covertly, the last of the old China and the beginning of the new. Prince Tung set down his teacup. There was one thing which each of those two shared in common — admirable self control.

"Mr. Moto was graciously explaining," Prince Tung said. "Now that he is apprehended the result can only be highly serious. It does not seem to me possible that Mr. Moto, or any of us, can be allowed to escape alive. If Mr. Moto comes free from here he will hardly forget the indignity. He and his government will pursue the man who insulted them like a mad dog. Americans may be insulted but not the

Japanese. If I were Wu Lo Feng I should certainly feel that the least embarrassing thing would be to dispose of all of us. I am sure Mr. Moto agrees."

Mr. Moto nodded. "Yes," he said. "I believe the Prince is right," and he smiled at me almost apologetically. "This, of course, is in my line of duty, but I am sorry that Mr. Nelson and the young lady should be here. I am very, very sorry. Affairs in the Orient are so complicated to-day. They grow so difficult, if you will pardon my saying so, please, because of the suspicions of your country, Mr. Nelson; and because of the suspicions of certain European nations regarding the natural aspirations of my own people." Mr. Moto spoke precisely and academically, as though he were lecturing to a class. "Yes," he said, "these suspicions make the most harmless activities of my country very, very difficult. A disturbance happens, anywhere in China, and my nation is always blamed for it. It is hard; very, very hard. Did not your own great country seize a large part of Mexico in the past century, Mr. Nelson? And what of Britain's colonizing efforts? The British Empire has always held out a helping hand to distressed and backward nations. Yet if my own poor country tries in the most altruistic way to settle even the smallest Chinese difficulty, there are notes of protest and inflammatory passages in the press. It is very, very hard. Believe me, Mr. Nelson, our policy at present is not to interfere in the internal troubles of China. We are scrupulously careful not to be identified in any disturbance, but you do not believe me, do you, Mr. Nelson?"

The conversation had been strange enough, as strange it seemed to me as the conversation at the Mad Hatter's tea party. First, there had been the tale of the tortoise outside the East Straight Gate, and now Mr. Moto was speaking earnestly, forgetful of his bleeding head, of the aspirations of Japan.

"Then why are you involved in this?" I asked him gently. "Why are you here this evening, with a broken head, if you are not interested in the internal affairs of China?"

Mr. Moto appeared momentarily embarrassed by my question. He frowned and drew in his breath.

"Shall we all be frank?" he suggested. "I cannot see what harm it will do to be frank. There is, Mr. Nelson, a disturbing, radical element in my country; even your great nation has disturbing political elements, does it not? There is a group in my country, somewhat bigoted and fanatical. It feels our nation is not moving fast enough. Frankly, this group has been a source of very bad annoyance. My mission out here has been to curb its activities. I am very much afraid that certain of my more radical, impetuous countrymen are instigating this Wu Lo Feng in the very bad step he is taking. Then there will be another incident, engineered by Japan, exactly what is so undesirable. Yes, I am afraid there are certain of my countrymen behind this. I have failed in preventing their rash action. Therefore I think that they will kill me. I do hope that you understand me now." Mr. Moto smiled at me brilliantly and then he added: "If they do not kill me, at any rate having failed I shall have to kill myself."

Prince Tung listened with mild and sympathetic interest, and looked thoughtfully at the dark shadows of the rafters.

"Mr. Moto has been most considerate to tell us so much," he said. "For my part, if there were not guards here, and if I had a sufficient length of rope, I think that I should strangle myself. It would be quite the most correct way out of this predicament. I have never felt so cold, uncomfortable or confused."

I spoke to Mr. Moto urgently, angrily, in English: "Moto," I said. "You are a man. You are a brave man. There are only two guards here. If we could get their rifles away from them we might do something."

Mr. Moto laughed and patted my arm affectionately. "I expected you to say that," he replied. "But excuse me, I am not feeling very well just now, and it would not do any good. The courtyard is full of men waiting to have weapons passed to them. Besides, do you hear the noise outside? I believe that our friend, Mr. Wu, will be with us in a moment."

The doors of the pavilion were thin enough to admit every sound outside. These sounds had told me long ago, without my being able to see, that there were a good many men lounging outside the doors. There was that peculiar undercurrent of coughing, chuckling, whispering and spitting which one associates with a patient and waiting Chinese group. It was the sound I had heard a hundred times before, in the yards of Chinese inns at night, when mule drivers and travellers gathered in small squatting circles around their teapots and their minute flagons of wine. It was the patient, orderly sound, like the background of everyday China, but it always had a portentous note, a half distinguishable undertone which might rise into hysteria and desperation only to return again to murmuring placidity. Now, as Mr. Moto reminded me, this lapping tide of talk outside, which had whispered in our ears like the sounds in the convolutions in a seashell, had changed perceptibly. A ripple of tenseness and excitement came from the courtyard into our dusky shed in an invisible, radiant wave. Voices grew louder, like the chatter of disturbed birds about to rise in flight. I heard several voices saying "Quiet," and everything was quiet enough outside, but still there was a change. I was listening, wondering what was going on, when Eleanor Joyce spoke to me.

"If Mr. Moto won't do anything you can count on me," she said.

"For what?" I asked her. She made a quick, impatient gesture.

"For helping to get out of here, of course. That suggestion you just made to Mr. Moto is almost the first concrete piece of common sense I have ever heard out of you. I am surprised that you didn't say that it doesn't matter, does it? Please try to be sensible. I haven't understood half of what you are saying. I suppose you have been trying to keep everything from me. Well, don't, I know enough. I can see that Prince Tung and Mr. Moto are scared to death, for instance."

Mr. Moto gave a horrified start. "Please," he said, "you are mistaken, please, it is not so. I be afraid? Oh no — please."

"No," I said. "Mr. Moto is not afraid, he only means to commit suicide. He is only afraid of being disgraced."

Eleanor Joyce snatched my handkerchief from Mr. Moto's hand.

"Come here," she said, "and let me tie this around your head."

"Thank you," said Mr. Moto politely. "Thank you very much."

"And now," said Eleanor Joyce again, "let's try to be sensible. If we know some facts we may be able to

193

do something. How can a lot of ragamuffins capture a large city like this, Mr. Moto? It's nonsense and I don't believe it."

Mr. Moto shook his bandaged head. I should have been amused by the conversation at another time. Even then it was momentarily diverting to see Eleanor Joyce's practicality encountering the unshaken logic of the Orient.

"Excuse me," said Mr. Moto, "American ladies are very impetuous. I know because I have observed them once when I spent a year in domestic service in your very lovely country, Miss Joyce. American women feel they can do everything. I think their men protect them perhaps too much. No, Miss Joyce, excuse me. I am so sorry to say that this idea of creating a disturbance is feasible. My investigations have shown it even before Major Best was about to call this matter to my attention. My investigations have taught me that the preparations here were very, very careful. I think that Major Best did most of it himself. He was once a very good member of the English Army Intelligence before he was made to resign."

Eleanor Joyce looked startled and I could sympathize with her, because the shade of Jameson Best had never entirely left me.

"What?" I exclaimed. "You mean to tell me that Major Best was in with Mr. Wu? He couldn't have been. He told me the other night — "

Mr. Moto touched my arm again. "Your people have a very nice word for it," he answered. "You have such apt words in your vocabulary. Double-cross I think you say, please. I think that Major Best was in partnership with Mr. Wu. He arranged the importation of weapons and of the selection of strategic meeting points. There were several maps in his desk, he was to be paid well for it. Oh yes, the Major would have been rich. Among other things he was to be given eight pictures. I think you know them please, Miss Joyce?"

Eleanor Joyce nodded.

"I am very, very pleased that you are interested," Mr. Moto said. "Major Best then had a thought, a nice thought. He thought that it might be better to sell to me also — so he might get everything — yes? Besides, I knew several things about the Major which might have made him unhappy. I think he would not have liked it if he had given me full information. He was about to tell me all arrangements and then he died. I am so very sorry."

"Never mind about being sorry. Go on," I said. It was a revelation to see Mr. Moto in such a loquacious mood and I know that he must have considered the situation hopeless to have told so much.

"Certainly," he continued. "I shall be pleased to go on, very, very pleased. You have a military word for what they do. Infiltration, is it not? For the last month Wu Lo Feng has had a concentration of disbanded soldiers at a spot out in the hills. A few of them have been coming dressed as peasants through the city gates, a few one day, a few the next. My people had suspected this for a long time but it has been very well done. I was able to acquire knowledge on the last of the arrangement only to-night, when I was struck on the head from behind. Yes, it is not nice. There are certain concentration points in the city. There are several field guns they have assembled in the Chinese city. At a given hour they will throw shells at the city wall. While the police are demoralized there will be outbreaks at several points. Wu Lo Feng himself will be in charge. You think it is audacious, yes? But it is very, very possible. There will be a great deal of upset, a very great deal of pillage. Before there is resistance, Wu Lo Feng — he goes. He runs away."

"Doesn't anyone know?" I asked. "The police must have heard something." Mr. Moto shrugged his shoulders.

"So many things have been talked about," he said, "so many things that no one believes. This will be an incident, I think, that is very serious. The Mukden incident will be nothing compared to it. Excuse me, I am very distressed."

Mr. Moto's anxiety was obvious enough to indicate that he was telling the truth and that he believed, that he was probably certain of, everything he was saying. I had lived in Peking when there had been fighting outside the city walls. I had danced more than once at parties in our foreign colony which had been held as a background of war lords' artillery fire. We had gossiped about war lords' proclivities at the Club, and had agreed that these things frequently happened but that there would be no disturbance in Peking. Somehow the peace of Peking was always accepted as an incontrovertible fact. Anyone who contradicted the idea was always scoffed at as an alarmist. We were all convinced that the dissensions of China would never touch us. We had been infected with the calm and the tolerance of the Chinese. Now that I was faced with the incontrovertible fact of an incident in the making, I had not lost my incredulity. I could see the complete logic of Mr. Moto's narration. I found myself classing it with another war lord intrigue. The only thing I could not believe was that I had any part in it.

"Do you know when this incident is going to occur?" I asked.

"Yes, approximately," Mr. Moto answered. "At an early hour in the coming morning, according to what I learn. I am very, very sorry that I could not know the hour."

"You mean to-night?" I repeated.

"To-morrow morning," Mr. Moto corrected me.

"And now, there is one thing you did for which I am very, very sorry. You struck Wu Lo Feng, with your fist, in the face, this evening at your house. Yes, I know of that also. I am very much afraid that you have too much temper. I am very much afraid that it is an affront which Wu Lo Feng will not forget. I think he will probably take you with him to the hills when he is finished here. I hope very much that you may be recovered before it is too late."

My tongue and my lips felt very dry.

"Thanks," I said. Although I had heard him, I still could not believe that I was in this predicament.

"But what will this man do with Mr. Nelson?" asked Eleanor Joyce. Mr. Moto coughed discreetly behind his hand.

"Please, perhaps it will be better not to think," he answered, "but you, Miss Joyce, you will be quite safe, I think. Wu Lo Feng will want so much to sell the pictures. He is not an ignorant peasant. Two hundred thousand American dollars will be valuable to him. Oh yes, of course, I know about the pictures."

Mr. Moto's suggestion that it might be as well not to speculate upon my future was smoothly and considerately put, but a difficult one to follow. I still could not be entirely convinced that I was the person who had incurred Wu Lo Feng's dislike by striking him in the face. Nevertheless, I could understand his point of view. He had been disgraced through my agency in the eyes of his followers. I had probably administered the form of disgrace which is most difficult to live down in the Orient. If our encounter had occurred in private he might have been eminently reasonable, but it had not. Both Eleanor Joyce and Mr. Moto were looking at me in a way that made me feel like a being apart. I tried to look unconcerned. I felt in my pocket for a cigarette.

"Well," I said, "it doesn't matter, does it?" But my remark was not convincing.

Then Eleanor Joyce asked a surprising question.

"But why?" she asked Mr. Moto. "Why won't he take me along too?"

"Please," said Mr. Moto. "There is really no fear of that. This man is really very sensible. Please, a merchant cannot be impolite to a customer. Oh yes! Everything will be very nice. You will be valuable to him safe, Miss Joyce." Mr. Moto bowed and turned to watch the soldiers by the door.

"Yes," I told her, "that's fine. It makes everything a lot better. Don't worry. Mr. Moto is generally right."

"No," said Eleanor Joyce, and there was a catch in her voice as she answered. "No, it isn't fine." But I did not ask her why because Prince Tung walked toward us, stroking his wispy gray mustache.

"I think from the noise outside," Prince Tung said, "that we are about to have a visitor. There are quite evidently a number of people outside, a crowd. You can hear them pushing. They are interested in us, I think. My ancestors were very strong men. I trust I shall not disgrace them."

I heard the sound to which he referred: a muttering, shuffling sound, like the noise made by an orderly crowd anxious to see an interesting spectacle. I heard someone outside give a low order. One of the guards was pulling open the side of the double door.

"Tom," Eleanor Joyce called to me. "Tom Nelson. I'm sorry if I've been nasty to you. I'm sorry."

She did not finish. There was a glare of white light which revealed a ring of faces staring through the open door. A man in blue clothes had entered, carrying a gasoline incandescent lantern, and the sudden intrusion of this white light was dazzling. It made the shadows of the pillars and the shadows of the religious mud figures dance. It made the doorway a spot of brilliance which framed two other figures walking through it as successfully as a spotlight on the stage. I knew the first one at once, although he was very much changed. It was the man whose acquaintance I had made in the courtyard of my house; it was Mr. Wu Lo Feng.

CHAPTER XIX

H E was no longer dressed in a servant's white gown. Instead, he was arrayed to present a figure which must have represented the fulfillment of his boyhood dreams. He was dressed as a military man, in a starched khaki uniform, with red tabs on the shoulders and red tabs on the high collar, probably a uniform which marked one of his periodic services with the armies of the early republic. A Luger pistol was hanging at his belt, with its holster flap cut away so that it might be drawn the quicker. His chest glittered with medals; I have often wondered what they represented. The uniform made him tall, taller than anyone present. It brought out the gaunt, athletic lines of his figure, but his face was just as I remembered it. His hatless closely shaven head gleamed with perspiration. His cheeks were sunken, haggard almost. His narrow eyes were puckered, like the eyes of a nearsighted man. The haggard look accentuated a lump on the side of his jaw. His mouth stood out from the face, with all the incongruity I remembered, that rosebud mouth of which Major Best had spoken.

The fallacy that all Chinese look alike has always seemed to me another of those myths which have gathered cloudily about that country ever since Marco Polo discoursed on its peculiarities. It is the same as the myth that Japanese tellers must be employed in Chinese banks because of the inherent dishonesty of the race. From another quarter it is said that Chinese tellers must be employed in Japanese banks for the same reason. Then there is the story of the conscientious Chinese tailor who copied a pair of trousers even down to the patch in the seat. These racial misconceptions are shared by the Chinese themselves. There is a universal belief in the less enlightened portions of the country, for example, that the knees of Europeans bend backward rather than forward. The belief that all Chinese look alike falls into a similar category. You would have been convinced of this if you had seen Wu Lo Feng that evening. There are different marks of character upon Oriental features due to different tradition — that is all.

Anyone who might have had the bad fortune to have encountered Wu Lo Feng that evening, with the white gasoline light clear on him, would have understood that he was observing a very exceptional man. The face, the bony face of generations of poor farmers, had been refined by inexpressible suffering and degradation into an example of exceptional survival. There was room for brains in the high, narrow, close-shaven skull. The eyes were frankly calculating, frankly curious, serenely unclouded by any civilized compunctions of conscience or charity. The jaw, in spite of the incongruous mouth, belonged to the man of action. It was the jaw of a Hindenburg, or a Pershing, or a Foch. I can think of Wu Lo Feng now as rather splendid, rather overpowering. When his glance met mine I felt distinctly shaky. It was an interested, probing glance and there were no words behind it. He walked into the centre of the room and stopped and his decorative lips pouted slightly, thoughtfully and mirthlessly.

His presence made one unaware for the moment of the man who was with him, exactly as one momentarily accepts the presence of the pilot fish about the shark behind the plate glass of an aquarium, without doing more than accept it. I remember that I had to remove my gaze with a conscious effort from the tall man in the khaki uniform to his companion. When I did so, I realized that his companion was also exceptional. He was a Japanese, dressed in a tropical worsted suit whose cut reminded one of an American business man's clothing. He was a man who was strange to me, and my first impression was of his physical frailty. His body must have been skin and bones beneath the worsted suit. The face, lined and nervous, was emaciated, almost skull-like; his upper teeth protruded over a receding lower jaw. It was the face of a man, probably a soldier, who had been severely, almost mortally, wounded once, and his left hand confirmed the impression. His left hand was badly deformed from some wound and was minus three little fingers, leaving only the little finger and a thumb. I remember that he held a lighted cigarette between the thumb and little finger. The frailty was not impressive in itself; there was a feverish glow in the frailty, a sense of will power inside it, that was burning that inconspicuous man like a high, perpetual fever. I can shut my eyes still and bring back the parchment like pallor of the tight drawn skin over his cheek bones. I can still see his uneven, protruding teeth. He was the first one who spoke. He spoke in the rather whispering voice of a consumptive, and to my surprise he spoke in English.

"How do you do?" he said and bowed. There is nothing in the world as perfect as a Japanese bow. There is a dramatic timing in the way the head droops that invokes an indefinable impression of courtesy and modesty and pride. His glowing, dark eyes were examining all of us, intently and enigmatically.

Mr. Moto was the one who answered. I had always thought of Mr. Moto as being a high strung man, but he was solid and adjusted compared to his fellow countryman.

"Good evening, Mr. Takahara," Mr. Moto said. "I thought you would be here."

Then I remembered. This was the man of whom Mr. Moto had spoken. So had Major Best. Mr. Moto did not say it was very nice. It was plain that Mr. Moto felt that Mr. Takahara's presence portended something diametrically the opposite.

"Yes, I am here," said Mr. Takahara. "In a few minutes you and I will step outside for a conversation, Mr. Moto. I am sure you understand."

"Yes," said Mr. Moto, "perfectly."

"I am sorry," Mr. Takahara said softly, "that we are not of the same political persuasion. And this lady and this gentleman — they are the two Americans? My name is Takahara, sir. I was in your great country once at the Washington Naval Conference. America and Japan are friends. I am sorry that a misunderstanding should be existing here to-night."

I bowed to Mr. Takahara and he bowed in return. Curiously enough, this exchange of courtesies did not seem out of place.

"Mr. Takahara is very kind," I said, "I am a great admirer of his country. I gather, Mr. Takahara, that you are one of the more advanced imperialists."

"Yes," said Mr. Takahara. "I am so sorry we have

no time to talk, because I have heard that you are a reasonable, interesting man. I am so sorry. Mr. Wu Lo Feng says that he will have need of you later. You and I are men of the world enough to know that accidents will happen. I am so sorry. I speak in English so that you will understand my position. Thank you."

"Thank you," I repeated.

Wu Lo Feng bawled out an order to the guards. His voice boomed jovially through the room.

"Why are these people not tied up?" he shouted. "Have two men to hold this foreigner. I am going to teach him something."

Mr. Takahara answered quickly in Chinese: "No," he said, "not now, General, you forget."

"Very well." Wu Lo Feng shrugged his heavy shoulders. "I can wait. This room will do. Bring in two chairs and a table and tapers. We will start off the messages."

Mr. Takahara raised his deformed left hand and examined a wrist watch.

"Yes," he answered, "this will do. Headquarters can be here, I think. There is not much time." Wu Lo Feng frowned at him. Two men were bringing in a table and two chairs. Wu Lo Feng let his belt out two notches, shifting his pistol holster on his side, and sat down. Mr. Takahara sat down also and the lantern was placed on the table between them.

"First," said Mr. Takahara, "we shall send runners to the mustering points. The arms will be issued; it is time to do so, I think."

Still frowning at Mr. Takahara, Wu Lo Feng leaned back in his chair, and again his voice boomed out:

"Please not to forget," he said, "I have conducted these matters before. You Japanese may control the provinces but I am not to be controlled. I can be hired but not controlled. Do you understand me, Mr. Takahara?"

"I understand you," said Mr. Takahara, "as long as you do what you have promised." Mr. Wu pursed his rosebud lips, his forehead creased with wrinkles, and he stared at Mr. Takahara insolently, with an active sort of dislike.

"Then do not talk," he said, "you are talking too much. You are annoying me and I do not like to be annoyed. You have seemed to be giving me orders to-night. Well, these men of mine take my orders and not yours. You are here as my guest. You are not even armed, Mr. Takahara. You are talking to Wu Lo Feng, who has seen more fighting than you have. I tell you again to be quiet. I am conducting this affair."

Mr. Takahara answered softly:

"Do not disturb yourself," he answered. "I never carry a weapon. I shall not forget anything you say."

Wu Lo Feng half rose from his chair and banged his fist on the table.

"And do not forget," he shouted, "that I am familiar with your methods. I know how far to trust you. You have given me money and assistance. That is all I have wanted. I know how to treat men who have betrayed me. Do you remember Major Best?"

"Please attend to the business you have undertaken," Mr. Takahara said, "and first, there are only two guards by the door. I should have more guards."

Wu Lo Feng laughed coarsely. He laughed and pounded his hand on the table. There was a reek of rice wine about him which told me that he had been drinking, but not to excess.

"They told me you were brave," he said, "and now I know they lied. You are a woman. You are afraid of this miserable countryman of yours, and of a debauched Manchu, and of an American woman and a man. If I had the proper weapons my boys could exterminate any Japanese Army that comes here. You think I am afraid with this courtyard full of former Chinese soldiers? No. I am not afraid. I have never been afraid of anything."

Wu Lo Feng looked at us and grinned. He had the bluster of a character in a Chinese play and I knew his type. I had seen war lords in Peking before; some had been small, quiet men but others had been arrogant egotists, exactly like Wu Lo Feng. He had all the overbearing pride and conceit of a self-made business man. He was the captain of his own industry and the master of his own soul.

"Yes," said Wu Lo Feng, "I shall conduct this business by myself. I know exactly when the guns you have supplied me will open fire against the wall. I know everything and there is time enough." Mr. Wu paused and rested his broad hands on the table. Anyone could tell that he was pleased with himself. He called to me by my Chinese name.

"Step nearer here," he said, "I think I can make use of you. I wish you to explain something to this woman, your countryman. You will tell her honestly what I say, I think. You do not wish her to come to any harm, I think. Many of your women are very delicate. Once, some years ago, I captured three Russian women when I raided a town to the North. They were not beautiful. I think all your women are very ugly but I saved them out of curiosity. I had to kill them finally because they could not stand the travel." He looked at Eleanor Joyce and then looked back at me. "Tell her truthfully what I say, please," he said.

I looked at Wu Lo Feng carefully. I was anxious to learn as much of him as I could because there is always a chance at such a time that something may be gained by temporizing talk. The most dangerous situations in China sometimes evaporate mistily in a cloud of words.

"What do you wish to tell the young woman?" I asked him.

Wu Lo Feng grunted. It has been said that there is always a touch of the shopkeeper in a Chinese bandit; as he framed the words of his next speech his manner grew suave.

"I wish to tell her nothing that she will not like," he said. "It was due to your meddling that she is here at all. Did Major Best tell you of the pictures? He demanded them in payment for his work; then he turned traitor. The young virgin wishes to buy them. I am pleased to have her buy them. Money is important to me. This life of mine cannot go on forever. A man in my position must retire. In a year, I trust that I shall be safe in Shanghai with sufficient property. I wish the money for those pictures, which I understand are very good. Mr. Pu is already looking for them. If he cannot find them I think Prince Tung will tell us where they are. Will you not, Prince Tung?"

Prince Tung nodded slowly. He also had been watching Wu Lo Feng.

"They are in my storeroom," he answered. "Yes, I have no doubt that Mr. Pu will find them. You will want ransom money from me, I suppose. I shall be relieved to learn how much."

Wu Lo Feng considered the matter. As he did so I remembered what Major Best had said that Wu knew exactly what he wanted.

"We shall all move to the hills in the early morning," said Wu Lo Feng, "you and Mr. Nelson both will go with me. We will discuss ransom there." He smiled slightly. "I offered to give Mr. Nelson a dinner last night. There would have been poison in it. Tonight I shall give him a better dinner when we get to the hills. I shall cook a piece of his flesh with my own hands. You have heard the custom, Mr. Nelson?" I knew that I should not have a pleasant time with Wu Lo Feng, but I was not sure that he would go as far as that. I did not answer. I even endeavored to appear indifferent because I knew it would be dangerous to betray any anxiety or fear.

"You will not wish the young virgin to go to the hills, I think," said Wu Lo Feng.

"No," I answered. "On the whole it would be better not." Wu Lo Feng grunted again and fiddled with the butt of his Luger pistol.

"Then tell her that Mr. Pu is coming with the pictures," he said. "Mr. Pu will lead her out of here to a place which is safe and comfortable. In fact, I think she may go back to her hotel before morning. Mr.

Pu will collect the money for the pictures. There is no reason for her to remain here. Tell her that I have no wish to hurt her. That will do. Take her to one side and tell her."

I walked toward Eleanor Joyce and took her arm. My respect for her was growing; she was holding herself well in control. She had been examining General Wu as though he were a figure in the circus. He was certainly as far removed as that from any type which she had ever seen. She was watching his hands as he toyed with the butt of his heavy Luger pistol.

"Come over here with me," I said and I tried to speak as casually as I could. "It's just what I thought. Everything is working out nicely for you. No one intends to harm you at all. Mr. Pu is coming with the pictures; then he is taking you away. You will be safe at your hotel by morning. You're out of this and I am very glad."

Her eyes looked as though she had not slept for a long while. She seemed to look straight through me.

"What will happen to you?" she asked. I tried to smile but I made a rather poor attempt at it.

"It really doesn't matter," I said. "Mr. Wu is taking me out to the hills with him. Country air and a change of scene. Don't worry, I shall manage."

"You mean they won't let you go, when I go?" she asked.

"It wouldn't be very wise under the circumstances,"

I answered. "Mr. Wu has taken an interest in me, but you needn't worry." My hand was still on her arm. Her fingers closed over mine, unexpectedly, convulsively.

"Tom," she said, "look at me, Tom Nelson. You can tell Mr. Wu that I am going out to the hills too, and there won't be any money for his pictures unless he lets us both safe off. I'm not going to leave you. I won't."

It was the first time that I realized that I had been laboring under considerable of a strain. I realized it when she spoke. The self control on which I prided myself was going into the discard. My face was growing red, my voice was thick.

"Don't be a fool," I said. "You're out and you're safe out. At any rate, he won't let you go."

"Tom," whispered Eleanor Joyce, "stay here with me. Don't speak to him yet."

We had walked a good many steps away from the table. We were far enough away in that shadowy room to have the illusion of being away by ourselves. The light was softer there. The people we had left were framed by the gasoline lamp but we were in the dusk, watching everything for a little while as spectators in a darkened theatre watch the stage. The guards with their rifles were standing by the closed door — Wu Lo Feng and Mr. Takahara sat side by side at the table. Wu Lo Feng was writing messages

213

with a brush. Mr. Moto and Prince Tung were standing disconsolately a little distance off.

"Would you be so gracious," Prince Tung asked, "as to send for another pot of tea?"

Wu Lo Feng looked up abstractedly and shouted to the guard: "Send out for tea and wine," he bellowed.

I saw Mr. Moto move toward Mr. Takahara. My knowledge of Japanese was rudimentary but I heard him asking:

"Might I trouble you for a cigarette?"

And Mr. Takahara was saying: "It is a pleasure."

Matters were moving on smoothly as Eleanor Joyce and I stood watching that amazing scene. That somnolent Oriental scene of order had crept in upon it decorously, in a way that defied a Western comprehension. The pot of tea came in and a small flagon of hot rice wine. General Wu tossed off two small cups of it.

"Send messengers," he bawled. Three men entered and he gave them each a slip of paper. He and Mr. Takahara were discussing something. Mr. Takahara was looking at his watch.

"I tell you," Wu Lo Feng was saying, "everything is ready." Eleanor Joyce pressed my hand again.

"Tom," she whispered, "why do you just stand here? Why don't you say something? Isn't there anything to do?"

"No," I answered, "of course there's nothing to do. You are looking at a remarkable scene if you stop to think of it. You see a Chinese bandit sitting at the table giving orders to start rioting. You see a Japanese provocateur sitting beside him; you see another Japanese agent who doesn't want an incident to be precipitated — not now at any rate. You are seeing history, in a way. It's a strange world here, isn't it? A nightmare of a world. It will be something for you to think about when you get home. There are Mr. Takahara and Mr. Moto both working for Japan, one trying to force the hand of the government, the other trying to let things go more slowly; and Wu Lo Feng thinking about himself, and Prince Tung drinking his tea. Here come some more messengers. Listen to the noise in the courtyard." I looked at my watch. For some unknown reason neither my watch nor my money had been taken. It was a quarter before one in the morning. "Yes, it's an amazing scene," I said. I was talking more to reassure her than for any other reason.

"I rather think something is going to happen before long. There is no doubt about it. This is the real thing. See — he is sending out more messages and here come some more men for orders. They look like foreign educated Chinese."

While I had been speaking a stream of men had been padding in and out through the temple doors, most of them young and intelligent. Some were Chinese in European clothes, some were in the coolie blue denims. For nearly a quarter of an hour we stood there watching Wu Lo Feng give orders while Mr. Takahara listened and gave an occasional suggestion. There was no doubt it was the real thing. Then the room grew quiet again and the guards stood by the closed doors. Mr. Takahara looked at his watch.

"In a few minutes," I heard him say to Wu Lo Feng, "we must be starting. You have charge of the railroad station, I believe."

"There's time enough," I heard Wu Lo Feng say. "We will not leave here until we hear the gun." Mr. Takahara rose.

"There is a detail at my orders outside, I believe," he remarked. "Perhaps it will be as well for Mr. Moto and me to leave, if you will excuse us. I shall be back in a few moments. Are you ready, Mr. Moto?"

"Yes," said Mr. Moto. "Will you permit me to say good bye to Mr. Nelson and Miss Joyce?"

"Certainly," said Mr. Takahara, "as long as Miss Joyce does not understand."

"What are they saying?" Eleanor Joyce asked me.

"They are only talking politics," I said.

Wu Lo Feng poured himself another cup of wine. "Would it not be better," he asked, "if I took Mr.

Moto to the hills? There must be no shooting yet."

"Thank you," said Mr. Takahara, "there will be no shooting."

"Tom," whispered Eleanor Joyce, "aren't you going to do anything?"

Her words made an idea flash through my mind. It was probably valueless but at least it seemed worth trying. I was reasonably sure that if Mr. Moto went out the door that he would not come back, and I rather liked Mr. Moto.

"Perhaps I can try," I said, and I walked toward the table where Wu Lo Feng was sitting. They all seemed annoyed as I moved near them.

"Please," Mr. Takahara said, "there is nothing here that concerns you." I did not answer him. As I walked toward that brightly lighted table I seemed to be back in a courtroom at home about to propose a motion before the Court. Wu Lo Feng, with his wine cup and his Luger pistol, was the judge.

"One moment, please," I said. "Perhaps the General is forgetting something."

Wu Lo Feng pursed his lips and set his wine cup down.

"What?" he asked me. "What am I forgetting?"

"It is simply a humble suggestion," I told him, "but one which can do Your Excellency no harm. Mr. Takahara is, no doubt, paying you to create a disturbance in the City. Have you ever thought to ask Mr. Moto how much he would pay you if you did not create it?"

There was a moment's silence. Mr. Takahara half rose from his chair. Mr. Moto drew in his breath with a long, sibilant hiss. Wu Lo Feng frowned and then he smiled:

"That is an excellent suggestion," he said, "and one I had not thought of. Sit down, Mr. Takahara. Please sit down. You have a good mind for a foreigner, Mr. Nelson. No, I have not thought of that." Suddenly his shoulders shook and he gave a shout of laughter. "It is very amusing. I have not thought of that. How much will you offer, Mr. Moto? But no, it will not do. You would offer a great deal, but how should I get the money? No, it will not do."

I stole a glance at Mr. Moto. His head bobbed toward me in a hasty bow.

"Thank you," he said to me, "thank you very, very much. Your suggestion is such a kind one, but Mr. Takahara knows that it is not in my power to make an adequate offer, just as he knows it is not in my power to promise not to mention his activity if I should be allowed to go free. You do not understand the complexities of our internal situation and I am very, very sorry there is no time in which to tell you of them. Mr. Takahara and I belong to different parties, his more radical than mine which is now

218

in power. Mr. Takahara is very considerate. Mr. Takahara and I, unfortunately, can only do certain things. If I had the opportunity I should have to dispose of Mr. Takahara. Now he has the opportunity. Nevertheless, he is a very nice fellow, and we are both in a way loyal servants of our Emperor. Please do not blame him. I am sure that Mr. Takahara is very, very sorry for you also; but now that you are in possession of certain facts, Mr. Takahara must allow Wu Lo Feng to take you to the hills." Mr. Takahara rose and bowed.

"Thank you," he said, "Mr. Moto. Thank you very much. Of course, the young lady does not understand the Chinese tongue and she must not know of this. I am sure that Mr. Nelson understands. I think now that the young lady had better be removed at once to the safe place of which the General speaks, and that Mr. Moto had better come with me."

The voluble flow of Chinese conversation moved about me dizzily. The politeness, the entire lack of animosity, was on the whole the strangest part of it. With cold fact all around us we were exchanging compliments as though we were at an evening party, while Eleanor Joyce stood in the background watching. General Wu moved heavily and grunted.

"Wait," he said, "wait a moment. It would be better for nothing to alarm the young virgin, and she is very valuable to me. It is far better that she leave before we do anything." And then he shouted to one of the guards by the door: "Ascertain if Pu has come. If he has send him here at once."

Mr. Takahara looked at his watch. I remember the shadow that his thumb and little finger made on the table as he raised his wrist.

"There is not very much time," he said. "Three o'clock is the hour."

"Be silent," said General Wu, "this is my affair. At any rate, here comes Pu."

He was right. The door was opening and Mr. Pu was entering, walking slowly with a great cloth bundle in his arms, and one of the guards shut the door behind him. Mr. Pu was bowing and smiling. Although I had grown to dislike him, I was never more relieved to see anyone than I was to see Mr. Pu and his bundle. It meant, if I was not wrong, that Eleanor Joyce would be safe. Whether she liked it or not, she would be sent away with Mr. Pu; and after that I believed that everything would be much better. Mr. Pu came walking in, exactly as I remembered him in the past, not in the least like a criminal engaged in a difficult intrigue. He came in venerably, bowing and smiling and puffing under the weight of his bundle, much as I had seen him a dozen times before entering my own house with a bundle of his wares. He had all the obsequiousness and the merriment of a good Chinese salesman who is ready to bargain or to laugh or to expostulate or to weep.

"Excellency," he said, "everything has been very fortunate. We came upon the pictures without difficulty and upon some other objects besides." I heard Prince Tung sigh softly but he made no remark.

Wu Lo Feng rose from behind the table.

"Let us see the pictures," he said, "the light will be good if you unroll them upon the floor. We shall speak of the other objects some other time."

"Time presses," said Mr. Takahara. "There is no time."

Wu Lo Feng snorted rudely:

"Let us hear no more from you, please," he answered. "I am the one who says whether there is time or not, and I say that I wish to see the pictures. I wish to examine them because I desire to have the bargain correct. I wish to have no mistake. Unroll those pictures. One of those men with a rifle — . You there, Cheng, put your rifle down and fetch stones to lay on the corners. And you, Mr. Nelson, tell the young woman to stand here beside me so that she may see them better."

Mr. Pu was kneeling upon the floor, unwrapping his bundle exactly as he might have unwrapped it in my house at home. One of the guards was standing over him, helping him. He looked like a shop assistant now that he had leaned his rifle against the wall.

"Ah!" Mr. Pu was saying, "they are beautiful,

beautiful. I say without boasting that I have an eye for art. The work is beautiful, Your Excellency."

I walked past the kneeling old man and spoke to Eleanor Joyce. I wanted her out of this as quickly as possible. I was sorry that there was even a delay about the pictures.

"Wu Lo Feng wants you to stand beside him and look at them," I said. "And then, thank God, you are getting out of this."

She moved forward obediently but she answered: "Oh no, I'm not. Not if you aren't."

I remember thinking resignedly that she and I would part forever, quarrelling.

"Oh yes, you are," I answered. "You won't get your own way this time. They'll carry you out of here if you won't go quietly. You mean money bags to Wu Lo Feng."

"Tom," she said, "I don't care about the pictures."

"Don't argue," I answered, "it won't do any good."

There was one thing at any rate that satisfied me. She evidently understood at last that there are times when argument is futile, because she walked toward the table and stood beside Wu Lo Feng. There was nothing as far as I could see that anyone could do, except to be resigned. There was one guard at the door with his rifle and another with his rifle at easy reach. Any sound of a struggle would have brought fifty or sixty others. There was nothing to do except to stand and take anything that came. I could only think that Eleanor Joyce was being let out. In a minute or two now, she would be gone. That dull hopelessness which was settling over me actually kept my thoughts slow and tranquil. I still seemed to be dissociated from the realities and the implications of that scene. I recalled thinking how right I was that events turn men and that men cannot turn events. The dusky figures around the temple wall were as solemn as the Fates. All sorts of unseen things in the room seemed to be gazing down as I did into the circle of bright light, where Mr. Pu was unrolling the scroll pictures. Although the last thing which I wished to do was to look at them, it was impossible not to look.

They drew my attention from everything else, once my glance fell on them, and it was the same with everyone else in the room, I think. Everyone was looking at the pictures on the floor. Wu Lo Feng stood gazing at them, a little puzzled, as though he could not decide why they should be coveted. Eleanor Joyce, standing near him, seemed to have forgotten everything but the pictures. Mr. Takahara, on Wu Lo Feng's left hand, forgot to look at his watch. Prince Tung and Mr. Moto and I stood by ourselves about three paces off. But we were looking also.

Any foreign visitor, ignorant of the technique of Chinese painting and prone to be puzzled by its unfamiliar technique, would have known that those scrolls were the work of a master, because they had that sense of greatness which can speak to any race in any language. There is a saying in China that a picture is a voiceless poem; those pictures had a breathtaking voicelessness. Something rose from them which laid hold of the senses and called for silence. They conveyed the idealism of the man who had painted them, the thought which was behind his work seemed to fill the room with infinite peace. They were beyond war or rumors of war. They were abstractions that rose above cupidity or fear. They were the Sung interpretations of landscape, which have never been surpassed by any succeeding Chinese dynasty or by the artists of any other race. The scrolls were like the first one which I had seen, of mountains and misty waterfalls, of pieces of countryside familiar to any one of us, but the artist had endowed them with his own interpretations. The brush strokes conveyed thought in a way that was as subtle as the strokes that go to make up the Chinese characters. They spoke of that paganlike, naturalistic religion which one can hear in sound between the lines of Chinese poetry. You had a sense of the earth and the water gods, of the rain gods and of the spirits of the air. There was some element in that landscape which must have spoken to anyone. Perhaps to each in a different way, but at any rate it spoke.

The impression which those scrolls gave me was one which leaves no memory of exact detail, for the impression was too dramatic and too strong. It was the contrast which I remember best between the deep, lucid stillness of those pictures and the sordid, anarchistic motion around us. It did not seem possible that brush strokes on silk, the combinations of color and line should leave such an impression in such a place, yet I remember thinking that the breathless, brooding clarity was an attribute of the land and of the genius of its people; that bottomless tranquillity was a part of the mountains and the valleys of the almost endless land outside our city walls. It lay behind all the turbulence of the life, mystically, indelibly. It explained why one felt security even in periods of the greatest disturbance. I remembered listening to the city sounds from my own house at the hour of sunrise. There was always a roar of sound from a Chinese city, unfamiliar to the native of another land because the sound is human rather than mechanical. Yet always underneath that sound was the mystical silence of the pictures.

Wu Lo Feng stood peering down at them, wrinkling his brows and puffing through his rosebud lips. He was a strange corollary to the perfection of Chinese art, but I think he was swayed by it like the most ignorant of his countrymen.

"These are very cheap," he said, "for two hundred

thousand dollars." Mr. Pu, still on his knees, nodded obsequiously.

"Indeed," said Mr. Pu, "they are cheap at any price. They are the work of the Emperor Hwei-tsung himself. Look! One has only to read the inscriptions."

Prince Tung spoke to me sadly:

"You must agree with me," he said, "that these are far too beautiful to be looked upon by any but suitable persons. They have been the treasures of ruling houses. I have never shown them to you, because, although I value your friendship, I have been afraid that your cultivation was not great enough; and now they will be taken from me, to be stared at by pale-eyed ghosts of barbarians who do not even know how to walk or speak, if you will excuse my saying so. I can truthfully remark that this is the saddest moment of my life. Will you excuse me if I turn my back?" And Prince Tung turned away.

Mr. Takahara gazed at the pictures also. He spoke more to himself than to any of the rest of us.

"Such work should be in Japan," he said, "where it would be suitably cared for and properly appreciated."

"Yes," said Mr. Moto, "I am very, very much ashamed of myself that I have never heard of them until this afternoon."

"Well," I began. My mind was still on the pictures. I was pleased now that I had seen them, if only for a little while. I looked up from the floor toward Eleanor Joyce. "I shall tell Mr. Wu that you will be glad to buy them," I began, "and then — "

I stopped. I could not have finished that sentence if my life had depended upon it. My eyes were glued on Eleanor Joyce. I could not believe what I saw and I had no great wish to believe it. She was reaching out her left hand, cautiously but none the less certainly, in the direction of Wu Lo Feng. At first I believed that the gesture was unconscious, but it was not. She was reaching for the Luger pistol that hung in the holster from the General's belt. I wanted to shout at her to stop but I seemed incapable of speech. The time element was too brief to think of anything much. I can almost think of her moving slowly, but actually she must have moved very quickly. No one noticed her at that instant.

"Stop!" I wanted to say to her. "Stop! you fool!" But the words were choked inside me. It was too late to tell her to stop. No one noticed her until the last moment, when Mr. Moto did. As I say, this all occurred in an instant, though it seemed like a distorted, dragging length of time that I stood there, mesmerized, watching. And then I heard Mr. Moto draw in his breath sharply.

"Ha!" said Mr. Moto. "Ha!"

Wu Lo Feng had never conceived the possibility of such a thing any more than the rest of us, until

Eleanor Joyce was snatching his pistol from his holster.

"Tom!" Eleanor Joyce was calling to me. "Tom! Quick!" And she had Wu Lo Feng's automatic drawn in her left hand.

CHAPTER XX

THERE was no time to think what a fool she had been. There was no time to think of anything. Eleanor Joyce had been asking why no one could do anything and Eleanor Joyce had done it. In a single, impetuous, uncalculated gesture she had upset all the tenuous, emotional balances.

"You fool!" I was saying to myself. "Now we're in for it. You've finished everything. We're going to be killed." The worst of it was that there was no time for anything, no time for consecutive thought. Yet it is curious how alert one's senses are in such a fraction of a second. My observation had never been so keen; my impression of every detail was incontrovertibly distinct. It was as though a swiftly unrolling film had stopped, leaving all the actors poised and momentarily motionless. Wu Lo Feng was turning, probably in a flash though it did not seem so. His expression was one of incredulous astonishment, mingling with a ludicrous touch of insulted dignity. Mr. Pu on his hands and knees among the pictures looked like a grandfather playing with children in the nursery. The man who had been helping him was scrambling for his rifle. The guard by the door was holding his rifle ready; Mr. Takahara was moving; Mr. Moto was moving; I was moving. Prince Tung was the only one who remained still. I could hear Eleanor Joyce's voice calling:

"Tom! Tom! Quick!"

I was moving, not because I wished to, or even knew what to do, but because I was under a compulsion. I had to move. That first instant is clear enough but the next is always vague and beyond my powers of reconstruction.

"You fool!" my mind was still saying, "we're in for it now." But I must have reached Eleanor Joyce in the same instant. I have a recollection of snatching the pistol and of pushing her behind me. Then I was standing, pointing the pistol at the body of Wu Lo Feng. For a second time that night, unfamiliar though I was with its mechanism, I had a pistol in my hand. I was thinking that it was up to me to say something when I found that I was already speaking.

"Don't!" I was saying in Chinese. "Please not to move, Your Excellency." But Mr. Moto was moving. I had a glimpse of him from the corner of my eye. He had seized Mr. Takahara by the throat. He was pushing Mr. Takahara into a chair. Then I was speaking again; my mind was on the guard by the door.

"Excellency," I was saying to Wu Lo Feng, "tell your guard not to fire. I shall certainly kill you first."

Wu Lo Feng was a man who was used to action and accustomed to quick decision. His shaved head snapped around to the doorway.

"Wait!" he shouted. "Wait!" Then his head turned back to me. "Let everyone be still," he added. His head had moved but the rest of him was motionless. He certainly believed that I would kill him and I think that he was right. His forehead puckered into an incredulous frown and the room was very still. All that I remember hearing was Wu Lo Feng's deep breathing.

"This is most ridiculous," said Wu Lo Feng, "this is entirely irregular. Try to be calm. You are being very foolish."

I could agree with him that this was most irregular and entirely beyond my own abilities of prediction, but I was calm enough, probably out of stark terror. I have never been able to take much credit for my actions. They were all, I think, dictated by unadulterated fear. There was only one thing that was clear to my mind. In all probability I would be able to kill Wu Lo Feng before Wu Lo Feng had me killed, and Wu Lo Feng was balanced enough to recognize the fact. At the time my reasoning did not go any further, except that I was quite convinced that I would have no compunction in killing Wu Lo Feng. I definitely did not like him. I wanted to tell him that I did not like him. I wanted to tell him that he was a mad dog but instead I said:

"Walk over to that chair, Your Excellency. Draw it back from the table and sit down in it. I shall be standing just behind you."

Wu Lo Feng hesitated and our glances met. Beads of perspiration were making his round head and his whole face shiny. I thought he was going to speak, but instead he walked carefully to the chair and sat down. I believe he understood that I did not like him. I stood just behind him. I allowed the muzzle of his Luger pistol to touch the back of his scrawny, unwashed neck just at the base of his skull. He did not cringe away from it but I am sure he felt the coolness of the muzzle. I am sure he did not like it any more than I should have.

"Wait, you turtle's egg!" said Wu Lo Feng to the guard at the door. "Do not finger that rifle. Do you not see that this fool has lost his wits."

Then he was addressing me. He did not turn his head. "There is nothing you can do, you fool," he remarked. "You can kill me but you will certainly be killed. Try to calm yourself. Try calmly to consider the consequences of your actions."

His advice was undoubtedly good. I have never tried so earnestly to think calmly and consecutively.

"That is exactly what I wish to do," I said. "I wish

to think calmly, Your Excellency. Tell that man to set down his rifle. It makes me very nervous. Prince Tung, will you be so kind as to pick up those two weapons, and put those two men in a far corner, and make them both sit down."

I was thinking and Wu Lo Feng must have been thinking too; except for an occasional glimpse about me, my sight was concentrated on the back of Wu Lo Feng's neck and on the back of his shaven head. I could see the veins pounding in the back of his neck but his muscles were motionless.

"Can you listen to me calmly," Wu Lo Feng asked. The thickness in his voice indicated that he was not calm himself. "Your ancestors were turtles. Your grandmother was a fallen woman. Your male ancestors were carriers of filth."

I prodded him softly in the neck, not that his interpretation of my ancestry disturbed me. I should have been interested to have heard him at another time.

"And you were a love child," I told him. I was sufficiently diverted at being able to insult him to forget the potentialities of our situation. "Your parents lived on the offal from the city trash heaps. Keep your mouth closed unless you can be polite. Careful! Careful!" And I prodded him in the neck again. Wu Lo Feng cleared his throat.

"You are seized with madness," said Wu Lo Feng.

"Someone will come in here at any moment. My messengers, my lieutenants. Do you not realize I am here on affairs. If someone comes in it will be the end of you."

I had been thinking of a possibility that seemed obvious and certain.

"Just as soon as the door opens you will end," I said. "It only needs the pressure of a finger."

There was a pause. I do not suppose that the pause lasted more than a few seconds, although it seemed much longer. He was thinking, I suppose, and I know that I was thinking desperately, without being able to arrive at any conclusion except that we had reached a stalemate. In another incarnation I once had possessed the reputation of being a good negotiator and of having a facile way of reconciling disputes between contending parties. I tried to think logically and fast, embarrassed because the whole room was waiting. Eleanor Joyce was watching me. Prince Tung and Mr. Pu on the floor, the two guards, Mr. Moto and Mr. Takahara — all were watching me respectfully. I was relieved to see that Mr. Moto had thrust a handkerchief into Mr. Takahara's mouth, because Mr. Takahara was held by no bonds of loyalty or fear. Eleanor Joyce, by her impetuosity, had arranged it so that I was holding the destiny of everyone in that room in my hands, tenuously, temporarily perhaps, but nevertheless certainly. I centered my thoughts upon the single obvious point which existed. The point was that I could kill Wu Lo Feng. He was astute enough to share the same conviction. He spoke again in a different tone.

"Wait!" he said. "Wait! Let us endeavor to be sensible. I repeat to you someone may come in here at any instant. That would be bad for you and bad for me. I have been very careless. I did not suppose the young woman could commit such an indiscreet act. It was too irregular to be considered, but now I shall make you a proposal. I think I have seen enough of you. The odor of you behind me nauseates me. I shall be pleased to let you leave here safely."

"Will you," I asked him. "How do I know you will?"

"My word, of course," said Wu Lo Feng. "You will be sensible if you abide by my sense of mercy." He must have known that his promise was a feeble one and that his integrity could have no possible negotiable value, because he added, rather pathetically, I have often thought:

"I declare to you that I really mean it."

"Think of something else," I suggested, "or I shall think of something." I was still trying to think of something when Mr. Moto spoke, in English, softly, like someone in a sick room, taking great care not to upset the patient:

"Excuse me," Mr. Moto said. "There is one thing

235

which I think might be very, very nice. Mr. Wu Lo Feng will be reasonable, I think. If there is a demonstration to start at the railroad station, as my friend Mr. Takahara has said, there cannot be very many people waiting here. If Mr. Wu were to go to the door and open it and simply give the order for the men to start ahead — they will go in motors I presume — and if he were to add that he will follow in a moment and in the meanwhile does not wish to be disturbed, I think, don't you, that it would be very, very nice. Of course, you must be careful of him, very, very careful. Please, I believe you can do it. He will understand that he must be truthful I think. If you would rather, you may take care of Mr. Takahara, and I shall be so glad to try. It is, of course, a suggestion; but I think it would be very nice."

"Thank you, Mr. Moto," Eleanor Joyce said, and the sound of a woman's voice just then was pleasant. "I think it is a very good plan. I am sure that Mr. Nelson can arrange it. For an amateur he seems to be doing rather well."

"Yes," said Mr. Moto, "very well indeed. Mr. Nelson is very nice. I like him very, very much. And you, Miss Joyce, I like you very, very much."

"Get up," I said to Wu Lo Feng, "slowly. Now walk slowly to the door. Never mind the pictures on the floor. Walk across the pictures."

"Yes," said Eleanor Joyce, "never mind the pictures."

I walked just behind Wu Lo Feng, with a pistol prodded in his spine and I explained to him what he was to do.

"Or if you have any ideas, use them," I said. "I shall be glad to leave the details to Your Excellency. You must see by now how important it is to have people out of the way, and for us to be private here. If you do so you shall have my promise that I shall try to save your life."

Wu Lo Feng halted in front of the faded red woodwork of the door. He did not turn to look at me but he spoke emphatically:

"It is impossible," he said. "They will not understand."

"Think," I said. "Your Excellency is an adroit man. Major Best himself has told me so. Think, if you do not want to die like Major Best."

"It is impossible," said General Wu. "If everyone goes they will understand there is some mistake."

"Your Excellency," I told him, "must understand that there can be no mistake. Send away as many as possible and do so in a way which I can understand, because we must have completest faith in one another."

I have often lived over the moment when I stood

behind Wu Lo Feng when ne opened the temple door. I have lived over all the imponderables which surrounded us both. They have awakened me often out of a sound sleep, to leave me staring, frightened, at the dark. Wu Lo Feng was a brave man. I know of no people who have a greater indifference than the Chinese to a certain type of danger. Wu Lo Feng was desperate and capable. I was the only person who controlled his actions. Those depended entirely upon his opinion of me and thus I could only hope that he had a higher opinion of myself than I had. I could only hope that he still clung to a certain conviction that he was very close to death, and yet at the same time had a chance for life provided he did what I told him. I had given him my promise honestly. I could only hope that he believed in my promise sufficiently not to make a dash for safety. As it happened, he must have believed it. He began to open the door.

"Not too wide, Excellency," I advised him. "It would be better for no one to see me."

He did not open the door too wide. I dislike to think what wild temptations must have been running through him. I could feel his back quiver as I prodded it. Once I believed that he was going to make a dash for it. I am quite sure he was on the point of it but he did not. He opened the door and shouted out an order, calling a man's name, and I could detect no anxiety in his voice. It was as loud, as unmusical, as arrogant as ever.

"You may go ahead," he shouted. "Have my car made ready. I shall be leaving in a moment."

The man had a sense of psychology. He must have known that I would be relaxed as soon as I heard him speak, and that my attention would be more on his words than on him because the instant he spoke he whirled around, with one of those strange, snakelike gestures of the Chinese boxer and slashed a fist at me. I had never known that I could be so nimble. I must have jumped back as soon as he moved. I had contrived to get just out of his reach and we were standing face to face. My pistol was still levelled at him.

"I should not do that again," I said. "That was unfortunate, Your Excellency. Turn around slowly and close the door." I could hear him breathing in deep gasps as he closed it. The strain was beginning to tell on Wu Lo Feng. "And now," I said, "walk back to your chair, and don't startle me again. It will be better for us both."

Wu Lo Feng walked back and Mr. Moto addressed me as he did so.

"Very, very nice," said Mr. Moto, with a sibilant hiss like a tea kettle. "Oh yes, you did that very, very nicely. I think things will be a little easier now. There will not be so much strain. I shall not suggest anything more. I see that I can safely leave negotiations in your hands."

There is a time for action and a time for thought. There is a time when it is better to do something, even if it is wrong, than to hesitate and think. Although I knew we were on the verge of such an occasion, I found myself unready for it. The sounds outside indicated that a number of Wu Lo Feng's men were moving away in accordance with his orders. Yet I knew there would be others left. The desire to get out of that place alive was overwhelming enough to make my thoughts illogical; my mind leaped at possibilities vainly, like an animal leaping at the bars of a cage. The situation of my holding a pistol against Wu Lo Feng's neck was growing ridiculous.

"We must get out of here," my mind was saying. "We must all get out. But how."

Wu Lo Feng must have understood what was passing through my mind because he was probably wrestling with exactly the same problem. I think this is the only thing that he and I ever had in common, except perhaps a mutual and increasing dislike. At any rate, Wu Lo Feng added an idea to the maze of ideas which surrounded me.

"You are getting nowhere," he said, "and you can get nowhere. This whole matter grows ridiculous."

"Perhaps," I said, "but then neither are you getting

anywhere." As it happened I was to see that I was mistaken. I should have known that the element of time was playing in Wu Lo Feng's favor. I should have known that he would be thinking and I should not have given him time to think. I had sense enough to know that there were too many prisoners in the room and that the mesmerism of the pistol at Wu Lo Feng's head would not affect them all indefinitely.

Over by the mud figures in a distant corner, I could see the two raggedy guards crouching on their heels, with the sleek but venerable Prince Tung standing near them holding one of their rifles and placing his velvet slippered foot upon the other weapon. I was relieved to see that the guards seemed moronically, apathetically stupid, but already they were shifting doubtfully and restlessly upon their heels. In the centre of the room, where it was lighter, Mr. Pu still knelt, undecided, by his pictures. I had an idea that Mr. Pu was simply thinking which side to take, but in the meanwhile he was being careful not to be a disturbing element. Mr. Moto was holding Mr. Takahara, who sat relaxed and motionless, too motionless I thought, but that was Mr. Moto's business. Eleanor Joyce was standing near the ruined altar. She was stooping, picking up something. She was picking up one of the ropes with which we had been tied.

"That's right," I said. "Bring some of those ropes

241

to Mr. Moto. Take some others to Prince Tung and start tying those men by their hands and feet. Don't mind if you hurt them. Quick about it now. And you, Mr. Pu, roll up those pictures. I'll see that you are made rich to-night if you help me, Mr. Pu."

Mr. Pu looked at me carefully.

"Yes," he answered softly, "yes, my master."

Things were going very well for the next half minute, better than I could have hoped, and I believe it was that half minute which saved us. At any rate, it took that length of time for Wu Lo Feng to think of something. Eleanor Joyce was as efficient as a trained nurse in an operating room. She had tossed two lengths of rope to Mr. Moto and Mr. Moto was securing Mr. Takahara's arms to the back of his chair. He worked swiftly, with an expertness which I should have expected in a man of Mr. Moto's broad experience. Without a single waste motion, Mr. Takahara's arms were pinioned to the chair. The bloody handkerchief from Mr. Moto's head was tied securely over Mr. Takahara's mouth. There is a conscientious thoroughness and neatness about Japanese handcraft which was pleasingly apparent in Mr. Moto's work.

"And now," Mr. Moto said, seizing another length of rope and skipping across the room, "permit me to help you if you please, Miss Joyce." I watched him almost complacently. He was like an expressman strapping up a trunk.

242

"On your faces," snapped Mr. Moto to the guards. "Hands behind you." The guards were very obedient. They must have known very well that they were pawns in a game of chance. They sprawled upon their faces. Mr. Moto had just finished with the wrists and ankles of one of them, hissing briskly through his teeth, when an interruption came. There was a banging on the temple door. For a second I think the sound made everyone motionless.

"Excellency," a hoarse voice was saying outside, "Excellency." I spoke softly to Wu Lo Feng.

"Say you're busy," I whispered, "say that you do not wish to be disturbed."

Wu Lo Feng drew in his breath and I thought he was going to say it, but it was there I was mistaken. Wu Lo Feng's breath came out of him in a shout that made me start.

"Help!" he bellowed, "Murder!"

CHAPTER XXI

THE audacity of it was like a blow but my reflexes were instinctive. I remember thinking that I should keep my promise.

"All right," I thought, and perhaps I said it out loud, "you'll take what's coming," and I gave the trigger of Wu Lo Feng's weapon a sharp, convulsive squeeze. I was prepared for the shock of a report but nothing happened. That anti-climax was one of the worst experiences I have ever known. I heard my voice ring out helplessly:

"The damned thing doesn't work," and I heard Mr. Moto shrieking in a ludicrous agony across the room.

"Oh!" Mr. Moto was shrieking. "Please, please throw a cartridge into the chamber."

I do not suppose I could have managed to do that, even if I had had a half a minute to examine the mechanics of that Luger automatic. As it was, I did not have an instant. The world was falling down. Wu Lo Feng must have realized the condition of his weapon. It must have come to him belatedly that I had done nothing about it.

The door had burst open and a man in blue denims was standing there. I recognized him in that sickening, shameful moment. It was the man with the pockmarked face who had invaded the reception room at Prince Tung's. His face, in that second, was long with stunned surprise and unbelief as he gazed at the astonishing spectacle which confronted him. His hand was sweeping to his pistol holster; his mouth was opened soundlessly. I realized that he was hesitating to fire at me because Wu Lo Feng was half rising to his feet, affording me a momentary shield. The man did not fire. Instead, he sprang with a shout at Wu Lo Feng and me. There was a crash as the table tipped over; the gasoline lantern was a puddle of exploding flame. I saw Mr. Takahara hopping, with the chair tied to him, toward the open door. I had a glimpse of Eleanor Joyce running and slamming the door shut. I heard a rifle shot. It must have come from Prince Tung. Then Wu Lo Feng, the pockmarked man, and I were tangled together. I have a recollection of striking Wu Lo Feng's head with the butt of that unfortunate automatic. It could not have had much effect on his skull, however, because I heard him shouting presumably to his pockmarked officer:

"I can manage this one. Keep off of us, you fool. The others! Watch the others!"

I was down on the floor, kicking, clawing in a reek of unwashed bodies. Wu Lo Feng's thumb was groping expertly for my eyeball. My right hand was struggling at his uniform collar to get a hold of his wind pipe. I believe now that the thing which decided the issue was a purely unintentional thrust of my knee into the pit of his stomach. I remember thinking that I could not be capable of such crude actions. The breath went out of him like the air from an inflated balloon. I heard him gasping, gurgling for his breath, and then I shook him off me and struggled to my knees. As I reached to get my balance I felt the Luger pistol beneath my hand.

The oil lantern by the door was still burning; the gasoline lantern was still a puddle of flame on the floor, which danced as dizzily as my head. General Wu, fighting for his breath, was struggling to roll over. Mr. Moto was leaning over him with another piece of rope. The pockmarked man was lying on the floor, breathing stertorously, with one of the guard's rifles beside him. It occurred to me that Mr. Moto had struck him with the rifle butt and I found out later that I was right.

"Please," Mr. Moto was saying, "I have him, please. That pistol, lend it to me for an instant." He snatched it out of my hand, gave it a jerk and handed it back to me.

"Now it will fire, I think," he said. "Would you

be so kind as to see that Mr. Takahara is quiet by the door. It might be well to shoot him if it is necessary."

I was on my feet by that time. I remember even then being favorably impressed by Mr. Moto's calm politeness in the midst of that turbulent nightmare. For myself, I was far from being calm. In spite of the battering I had taken, I felt an exhilaration such as I have never known, a drunken, crazy exhilaration. I was a part of that vortex of motion. I was completely attuned with its speed. I should have been delighted to have killed anybody. I should have been overjoyed to have faced another physical encounter, and I believed that there would be ample opportunity in the next few seconds. Eleanor Joyce was standing, pushing against the door. I had a glimpse of a guard, lying bound and of another lying dead. Prince Tung, in his plum colored vest, holding a rifle, was bending over Mr. Pu.

"Do not be clumsy," Prince Tung was saying. "Pick up my pictures and be ready to carry them or I shall most certainly kill you. Mr. Nelson, I think we had better make our way out of here."

I agreed with him that it was time to get out if we ever were. I could hear them outside beating against the door, but Mr. Takahara is the one I remember best. His hands were still bound to the chair. He was still moving toward the door, half walking and half sitting, a hideous farcical figure, weak, emaciated, struggling with his gag. I should have felt sorry for Mr. Takahara if I had not remembered that he proposed sending me to be tortured in the hills. As it was, Mr. Takahara evidently expected no pity. When I approached him he tried to throw himself on me, chair and all, and I picked him up, chair and all, kicking, groaning, and tossed him backward out of the way.

"Moto," I called, "we'd better run for it."

"Yes," Mr. Moto called back, "I think that would be very nice. If you shout that the police are here I think that it might help. Yes, you must be going."

Then Mr. Moto was beside me, holding the other rifle. I had snatched Eleanor Joyce away from the door, Mr. Moto was pulling it open, his voice had risen to a high treble:

"The police!" Mr. Moto was shouting, "we have been betrayed. His Excellency is taken. Save yourselves! Police!" Then he lowered his voice: "Quickly," he said. "You first, Mr. Nelson."

At another time I should have thought my act was suicide. It was probably close to suicide then, although I was not in a fit state to weigh the chances. I was out of the temple door into the warm night, firing the Luger automatic. The darkness was not too heavy to obscure a line of roofs and buildings. I was on a raised terrace, with a marble balustrade, and a flight of steps before me led down a dark, conventional, temple avenue, past the black and shattered eaves of a bell tower and a drum tower to a gate. There were some men, not more than five or six, half way down the steps. I fired at them and they turned and ran. I suppose they were as confused as I was. When a leader is eliminated, Chinese are apt to run. What alarmed me most was the thought that they might be back in a minute, cutting loose Mr. Takahara and Wu Lo Feng. Eleanor Joyce was just behind me. I took her hand and ran down the temple steps. We did not have a very long distance to go because the temple, in spite of its conventional design, must have been a small one. We did not require much more than fifty steps to reach the main gate. There was a small doorway inside the great gates themselves.

"It will be bolted," I heard Prince Tung's voice say behind me. "Allow me, please." Prince Tung pushed past me. There was a grating of metal and the small door creaked open and we were out in the street. An automobile was standing without the gate. When I saw it I remembered that Wu Lo Feng had asked for his car to be ready. We had moved so quickly that the driver of the car could not have understood what had happened.

"Quiet," I told him. "Stay where you are." Then I told Eleanor Joyce to get in. Mr. Pu, with the roll of pictures, followed us and then Prince Tung. At this point I realized that Mr. Moto was not there.

"Moto!" I shouted, "Moto!" But there was no answer.

"Come," said Prince Tung, "we must leave him. This is very dangerous and I wish my pictures safe."

"No," I said. "I'm going back to get him."

I meant it, because Mr. Moto had been a good companion.

"Tom!" cried Eleanor Joyce, "you can't."

Then I heard someone running. Mr. Moto was jumping over the high threshold of the gate.

"Excuse me," he said. "I am so very, very sorry. There were some notes in Mr. Takahara's pocket. I am very, very sorry to be delayed, but I have the notes and they are very nice. Quickly. Tell that man to drive on." And he pushed into the driver's seat beside me.

"Yes, the notes are very, very nice," Mr. Moto said. "They tell me what I wish to know. I think we can arrange everything now. I think it might be well to drive towards your house. If you will be so kind as to drop me at a point I designate I shall be very, very grateful. Then I shall rejoin you at your own house if you will be so kind as to let me use your telephone."

"Certainly, Mr. Moto," I said, "it will be very, very nice."

Mr. Moto laughed nervously:

"Thank you so much," he said. "Yes, on the whole it has been very, very nice." And he tapped a little notebook he was holding in his hand.

I have never known exactly what Mr. Moto did, because it seemed a wiser policy not to ask. It was not hard to conclude that the intricacies of secret service and of police were much better without my curiosity. I had seen enough of them at any rate that night. The only thing I am certain of is that Mr. Moto knew exactly what to do.

The thing which impressed me most was the quietness of the streets that early morning, although the quietness may have been a simple contrast that was only rendered emphatic by what had gone before. It seemed incredible that there was no stir upon the streets, or the slightest echo of the imminence of trouble. Yet there I was sitting beside a frightened driver with a pistol in my hand, while Mr. Moto gave an occasional curt direction.

Once he said: "There is ample time I think." But this was the only indication he gave of having anything on his mind.

There was no daylight; warm darkness covered a city that was moving lightly and lazily in its sleep, for Peking is always moving even in its dreams. The occasional electric street lamps on the broader ways picked out the fronts of shops, shuttered except occasionally where an eating house was open. A few shadowy figures moved silently around the city walls. The night soil carriers were already beginning to stir. There was the clatter of a watchman's rattle down some invisible back alley, warning draw-latches and thieves that the law was awake and alert. We turned into the square known as the square of the four Peilos because of four carved wooden arches which spanned four converging ways. Their decorated posts rose up from the street lights around them into the warm black of the sky.

"We will stop here please," Mr. Moto said. "I shall get out here, please."

I told the driver to stop and the car stopped.

"Moto," I asked him, "do you want any help?"

Mr. Moto stood by the running board; the gold fillings of his teeth glittered in the rays of the street lights. I wondered if I looked as badly as Mr. Moto did. His collar was torn, his necktie was askew, one side of his coat had been ripped, one side of his face was swollen and the whole of his face was grimy from his wounded scalp.

"Oh no," said Mr. Moto, "no, thank you very much. I had discovered nearly everything before I was so unfortunately caught to-night. I shall know exactly what to do, thank you. Now if you please, I must give you some directions. The City will be under martial law in a very few minutes I think. Then no one will be allowed upon the streets without a pass. That is why I suggest you go home at once. You may leave the driver and the car outside. He will be taken care of. There is nothing for you to think about. . . . Nothing. But may I come to you as soon as a few small affairs are arranged? It would be so very nice. And then perhaps we may have some whiskey. Ha! Ha! Good whiskey for good friends. Thank you very much."

"Thank you," I answered, "thank you, Mr. Moto."

It occurred to me that I did not know exactly what I was thanking him for, although I felt very grateful. My main feeling just then was one of amazed respect, and I was convinced that he was one of the most remarkable men that I have ever known and certainly one of the most capable. Eleanor Joyce held out her hand to him and Mr. Moto drew his breath politely through his teeth.

"Thank you, Mr. Moto," she said.

"It has been a pleasure," Mr. Moto answered. "Now will you hurry please?"

CHAPTER XXII

WE rode a long while without speaking; no one spoke again until the car had reached my house. A dull lassitude of reaction was coming over me so that I did not wish to speak. I was content to keep an eye on the driver and to examine the dark streets, while my mind juggled idly with a series of unrelated thoughts. I thought of all the other times when I had travelled home through Peking in the small hours of the morning, in motors or in rickshas. I thought of the gayety I had known in those small hours and of the kindliness and the tolerance; Peking is perhaps too tolerant and gay. I thought that it was strange that this home-coming had many of the aspects of those others. I was lulled by the same sense of security and well-being, although I knew that it was false. That side of China which lulls every foreigner into carelessness until he becomes soft and useless was caressing me again. I was lapsing back already into something which I had been before that night. Already my activity in the last few hours was assuming an undignified and an unprepossessing aspect, until I thought with a sudden twinge that Mr. Taka-hara and Wu Lo Feng were not so far away. They would be untied by now. They were not the type of person to forget. I was glad that Mr. Moto had promised to come back when his business should be over.

We were coming into the narrow alley where my house stood and I had just told the driver to stop, when I had concrete evidence that Mr. Moto had been busy already. Just as the car stopped beneath an old willow tree that stood beside my door, two men moved out from under its shadows who wore the khaki uniforms and the white belts of the Peking police.

"It is all right, Excellency," the other said to me. "We have been told what to do with the car. Will you please all to get down?" He walked with me politely up to my front gate and beat the iron ring down hard. My own gatekeeper opened it just as he had on a hundred nights before, but for once I think he was surprised to see me — surprised and almost agitated.

"Master," he began and stammered, "we did not expect you, Master."

I remembered the last time I had seen him, when Wu Lo Feng and his men were there, and I was surprised that he was still alive.

"There is no one here besides you, of course," I said.

His answer was prompt and confusing.

"Oh no," my doorman answered. "It is not so. Everyone is back, but it is regrettable. I do not think they expect the master. I shall tell them, please."

"You shall tell them nothing. You shall stay here," I said, and Eleanor Joyce and I walked past him, with Prince Tung and Mr. Pu following just behind us. The gatekeeper still stared at me. His glazed eyes reminded me that I was still holding the pistol in my hand and that I probably was a shocking sight, but there was more than amazement in his stare. The man was acutely embarrassed.

"I shall go to tell them," he repeated.

"No," I told him again, "you will stay right here."

I was ready to expect something strange when we walked around the spirit screen and through my little garden and through the pavilion where I ate into the second courtyard on which my library and my bedroom faced, but I was not ready for what I saw.

The library was brilliantly lighted. My number one boy Yao was inside and also my cook and my assistant cook, my ricksha boy and my yard man. They were wrapping all my possessions into cloth bundles, my clothes, my books, my bric-a-brac and bedding. Just before Yao saw me he was examining my dinner jacket. When he saw me he let it fall to the floor. I understood what he was doing and he knew I understood. Through one of those channels of intelligence so peculiar to a Chinese servant, Yao must have learned what had happened to me. He must have been very certain that I would never come back. He was taking the occasion to remove my personal effects; and a man of another race might have been confused on being discovered. I never admired Yao as much as I did at that crisis. We gazed at each other quite calmly over the bundles of my clothes.

"Your mother in the country is better, I suppose," I said.

"Thank you for your graciousness in asking," Yao answered. "It is true that my mother has fortunately recovered her health and I returned instantly to be of service as always to my master. We have all returned. We were alarmed at news that there might be some trouble. We have been hastening to pack the master's possessions, to convey them to a place of safety."

We both knew that there was more to it than that. I was disappointed in him because I would have staked my reputation that he was a faithful servant.

"So you thought I was dead," I said.

And then his composure left him. I shall always remember his explanation because it was logical, like so much of the Chinese mind.

"Master," said Yao, and I knew by his tone that he was genuinely hurt, "surely the master knows that I should be proud to serve him to the death while he was alive. Surely the master would not have objected to my disposing of these things. The clothing would have been valuable to no one else. The other effects I should have saved of course. Surely the master understands me."

I understood him. I felt kindly toward him again. As a matter of fact, he was absolutely right. There would have been no use for my things after I was dead. I should have been pleased to have allowed him to make any use of them which he might have seen fit. Furthermore, I am convinced that he would have served me without pay indefinitely, as so many Chinese servants have served their European masters, as long as I was alive. It still seems to me that Yao was a perfect servant, and that I shall never know a better. I still do not know why that incident made a disagreeable impression upon me. A day ago I should have accepted it all with tolerant amusement, but now I was not entirely amused. It may have been because I was face to face with a posthumous sort of reality.

"I understand you," I said. "You would have been welcome to everything, but now of course everything must be put back. And you forget yourself. I have guests here who are tired."

Yao understood me at once. He shouted to the other servants.

"What are you staring at, you clodhoppers?" he shouted. "Do you not see the master is back with guests? Set this place to rights. Go to your places and prepare him food. Do you not see the master is fatigued? Bring the whiskey and soda. Bring tea. Place a chair for the lady. If the master will come with me I shall get him clean clothing. I shall bring the lady warm water."

"Yao will look after you," I said to Eleanor Joyce, "if you will go to my room. Yao is an excellent servant. We shall have something to eat in a little while. I am sure he will make you comfortable."

Eleanor Joyce looked at me and smiled. "Yes, I'm sure he will," she said. "Thank you. You've been very kind to-night. I've always known that you were kind."

I have never known that my servants could move so rapidly and so efficiently. The cook and his assistant had disappeared into the kitchen. The ricksha boy and the yard boy were putting back my books and ornaments. Yao was bringing whiskey and soda bottles. In almost the same moment, so fast did everything seem to move, he was offering tea to Prince Tung and Mr. Pu. He was bringing us towels soaked in hot water. He was helping me into a new coat. The old life which I had known and loved was coming back around me, but somehow it was not the same. Somehow I knew that it would never be the same again. I felt as I had not felt for years, that I was a stranger in my own house, that I was a member of a different race, unable to cope with the suavity around me, unable to trust anyone fully, unable to rely on the loyalty of anyone except perhaps Prince Tung. I knew that I must even distrust Prince Tung himself within limits. Prince Tung had seated himself in one of my chairs and was sipping his tea while he surveyed the disorder of the room. Mr. Pu had laid down his bundle of pictures and was bowing to me ingratiatingly. He knew that I recognized all his deviousness, but we were passing it over as we passed over anything that was unpleasant, as we passed over filth and corruption and the hideousness of beggars and starvation and human degradation.

"The tea is excellent," said Prince Tung, "and very refreshing." And he glanced toward Mr. Pu. "I think," he added, "now that this fellow has brought the pictures here we may have no further use for him. I suggest your servants beat him and throw him in the street."

Mr. Pu gave a cry of pain and astonishment. "Excellency," he cried, "is it fitting to say such things? When I have done nothing but serve you, when I have risked my life from devotion? Besides Mr. Nelson has promised to give me money. I know that I may rely on his integrity. Besides, if I am placed in the streets there may be trouble. I have done all this solely on behalf of Your Excellency." The man was a snake in the grass and he knew I knew it. I reflected at the same time that there must be millions like him.

In a land where existence was so difficult, where all things were so unstable, there would be a million like Mr. Pu.

"You will be taken care of," I said. "Go out to the kitchen and tell them to give you food and give you some place to sleep. I will speak to you in the morning." Mr. Pu clasped his hands in front of him and bowed, as he might have bowed to a holy man.

"The master is gracious," he said. "I shall always be his grateful slave."

"Go," I said. And Mr. Pu disappeared into the courtyard.

Prince Tung smiled faintly. I turned to a low table where the whiskey and soda stood and I heard his voice above the soda water as I poured it into the glass.

"My country," said Prince Tung, "is an interesting country. Do you not agree with me?"

"Yes," I said politely. The whiskey made me feel better. I had never needed a drink so much. "Your country will always be the most interesting country in the world."

"Yes," said Prince Tung complacently, "and the most advanced, and the most intelligent, I think."

"Too intelligent," I said. Prince Tung smiled again.

"Exactly," he agreed. "It is acute of you to understand. If you had come here as a younger man and had been given the proper teachers I think you might have been entirely sympathetic. You are quite right. We are too intelligent. We have forgotten nearly all that you are learning now."

"Also," I said rather rudely, "you are the most insufferably conceited people in the world."

"Are we?" said Prince Tung. "I do not entirely understand you. We are certainly the most logical. I doubt if any one of my countrymen would have made such an unconsidered and foolish gesture as your countrywoman did to-night when she snatched the pistol from an armed man's belt. It was an incongruous gesture and one which had no reason to succeed. It is such sudden insane bursts of your countrymen which make it so difficult for us to understand you."

"If she hadn't done it, we wouldn't be here now," I said.

"That is true," Prince Tung agreed, "but then logically we have no right to be here at all. And there is another point," Prince Tung looked at me accusingly. "You also disappointed and surprised me to-night. You also acted illogically, in a way which I cannot resolve. You, too, exhibited that strange lack of reasoning so inherent in your race. It is beyond me to understand how you can be a great people."

"And what was my fault?" I asked him.

"Can you be serious in intimating that you do not understand?" Prince Tung demanded. "Yes, I believe you are serious, which is only the more confusing. Just before we left that room where we were imprisoned, you had an opportunity of performing an act which would have been highly useful to everyone. You had a weapon in your hand. Why did you not use the weapon? Any right-minded man would have done so. You should have killed Wu Lo Feng the moment before you left. He himself would have understood it perfectly. He certainly expected it."

The placid glance of Prince Tung was mildly accusing and mildly incredulous. More than that, I could interpret a polite contempt in the Prince's look. I had fallen in his estimation. I had been tried and I had been found wanting. Although I argued the point with him, I knew there was no use. At least I had the sense not to put my defense on the grounds of humanity because I knew that such an explanation would have been beyond him.

"I could not kill him. I had given him my promise to try to keep him alive," I said. Prince Tung placed his hands squarely on his knees. His attitude was changing from contempt to charitable benevolence.

"Surely," he said slowly and politely, as though he were afraid that I might not follow him, "surely you should have known enough to have understood that such a promise has no validity, when counterbalanced by practical advantages. Wu Lo Feng himself placed no faith in such a promise. You should have killed him. You would have saved yourself difficulty and danger. By not doing so you have alarmed Wu Lo Feng."

"Alarmed him?" I echoed stupidly.

"Yes. Alarmed him very much," Prince Tung replied. "Now he knows that he cannot rely on you to be logical. He knows now that your existence is a perpetual source of danger to him. He knows that you will try to have him apprehended. Yes, he will certainly try to kill you, now that you have shown him mercy."

In spite of myself, Prince Tung's ideas made me uneasy, because Prince Tung was nearly always right in his estimate of the characters of his countrymen. It occurred to me that Wu Lo Feng would be at large by this time, and that nothing would be very safe for me either in the city or beyond the walls. The impersonal, liquid voice of Prince Tung made me want to answer him sharply. I was learning, as every foreigner must sometimes learn, that I was incapable of coping with Oriental complexities. The vagaries of Prince Tung had delighted me once, but now they only added to my growing exasperation. My own deficiencies and his were clear enough that night to show me that a mutual understanding was nearly hopeless. An idea passing through the mind of Prince Tung warped itself like light travelling through a lens and dissipated itself mystically into a hundred lesser lights. Yet none of these disturbed the crystal clearness of his inner conceit and tranquillity. I was about to answer him when Eleanor Joyce returned. I was glad to speak to her instead because I knew that she would understand me.

"Prince Tung and I were making some philosophic observations." Eleanor Joyce had been looking at me in a friendly way but now her face clouded.

"Haven't you talked enough about that?" she asked. "Are you going right back where you started, Tom? Are you going to go back to talking?"

"Perhaps you are right," I said, "but I thought you might be interested. Prince Tung was saying that it was most irregular for you to snatch the pistol from Wu Lo Feng."

Then Eleanor Joyce smiled. She was beautiful when she smiled.

"At any rate it made you do something," she said. "It was probably the first time you were ever obliged to do anything definite for years. At any rate you might be obliged to me for that."

"I think perhaps I am obliged to you," I said. "I'm not exactly sure." I was not entirely sure of anything now that she was speaking, except that I was pleased that she was back. There had been a definite sort of antagonism between us, but now it had disappeared inexplicably. Without having any basis for my conviction, I knew that we were friends — very good friends, as Mr. Moto would have said. Nothing about her irritated me any more. I knew that I had changed in her estimation also and I was grateful for it.

"And you did very well once you started doing something," she said. "Once you did something besides talk and say that it doesn't matter." Her glance was steady and kindly but not her voice. "I respected you a good deal to-night, more than I've respected any man I think. You were brave to-night." I tried to answer her carelessly as I would have a few hours before.

"Anyone would have been brave under the circumstances," I said. "Let's forget about it if we can. It was rather a ridiculous piece of business." Eleanor Joyce shook her head.

"I don't agree with you," she said. "There are some things I shall be glad to remember always." She smiled again. "You might give me a little of that whiskey, please," she added.

I still tried to answer her carelessly but the attempt was not a great success. Although I was under no illusions about myself, something had changed in me which I could not estimate and I wondered if she was speaking of that change.

"Thanks," I said. "You are kind to put it that way. But just remember that no one can be sublimated very long. Circumstances make one move in certain ways."

"But you moved circumstances," she said. "We both did, didn't we? At least I have taught you that."

"What?" I asked her.

"At least I've taught you that it isn't always worth while to drift. You can be as much of a fatalist as you like, but don't forget there are times when you can do something. There are times when anyone can make fate change a little. Men have done a good deal to change the world. You and I have changed it a little. People may be altered by circumstances but they can alter circumstances too. At any rate I've taught you that."

I did not answer her. I had not thought of matters in exactly that light. I tried to cast back to possibilities, wondering what would have happened if she had done this and if I had done that. I tried to make an estimate, but all such speculation is useless. And then she spoke again.

"Tom," she said, "you're not going to go back, are you?"

"Back where?" I asked. I did not understand her.

"Back to where you were when I found you," she said. "Back to doing nothing but sitting, to talk amusingly, back to escaping from everything that is actual, back to being waited on and quarrelling with servants, back to being an expatriate. You are not going to do it, are you, Tom? You're better than that, you know."

I was neither indignant nor cynical when she asked me, although I should have been one or the other a little time before. I could see rather clearly what she meant, perhaps too clearly to be comfortable. I remembered what a business man in Shanghai had told me once, who had considered himself an old China hand, although he had hardly moved beyond the limits of the Treaty Ports during his years in China. He said that his company had always discouraged its young men studying Chinese or learning Chinese customs because such interests invariably made men queer. I had been intensely amused at this theory at the time, I remember, but now I found myself wondering if perhaps he was not partly right. I wondered if I were growing queer. I wondered if anyone brought up in one tradition could ever assimilate another without losing a certain balance of integrity.

"Tom," she was saying, "you aren't going to, are you, Tom?"

"I understand what you mean," I said, "but my answer is, I don't know. After all it's rather hard to change. At any rate it doesn't matter, does it?"

"Doesn't it?" she asked me, "I rather hoped it might."

I was relieved when Prince Tung interrupted us. Even if he had understood English I doubt if our conversation would have interested him.

"I hope," said Prince Tung, "that the young virgin is speaking about the pictures."

"What pictures?" I began. I had forgotten almost entirely about the scroll paintings. "No, she is not speaking of them."

"Then it is high time she should," said Prince Tung. "They are here. I consider them a matter of very great importance."

"Prince Tung is asking you about the pictures," I said to Eleanor Joyce.

"The pictures?" she asked. And she looked as though her mind were on something else. "It is just as well he spoke of them. I am not very proud of what I have done about those pictures. I understand a good deal more about them than I did. Tell Prince Tung I had no idea they were going to be stolen from him. Tell him I am very much ashamed. The pictures are his, of course. Tell him I should not think of trying to buy them from him. They should be owned by someone like Prince Tung. I can understand why you did not like it when you heard I was trying to buy them. You see, I never really knew what it implied. I am sorry about it, Tom. I am through with all that, really. I am a sadder and a wiser girl to-night."

I was pleased with her reaction. I knew that I had something to do with her making that decision, and it seemed to me eminently a just one. If she had changed me momentarily, I had changed her also.

I explained the matter to Prince Tung, delicately, eloquently, because, I thought, being a man of essentially cultivated instincts, that the Manchu nobleman would share my pleasure. I wanted him to see that we were not all barbarians, not all of us bent on pillage. As I explained, I was surprised to see Prince Tung puff out his cheeks and exhale his breath loudly.

"What?" he said. "She does not wish to buy my pictures? But this is quite impossible."

"No," I answered patiently. "Miss Joyce has delicate sentiments. Foreigners sometimes have, Your Excellency; not frequently, but sometimes. There are some of us who do not wish to take what is rare and beautiful from your country. Some of us—but not many."

"But this is impossible," said Prince Tung again. "It is beyond all the lines of logic. A little while ago she desired the pictures. What has happened to them since that she does not desire them? This is very terrible. This is distressing. I begin to be ill. It is essential that she buy my seven pictures for one hundred and seventy-five thousand American dollars."

I stared at the Prince, without speaking, because his reasoning was beyond me.

"Why?" I asked, at length.

"I do not see why you have to ask," said Prince Tung almost testily, "for a simple explanation. If she does not take these pictures every thief in the City will know of them now. Every thief in the City will break into my wretched house, as they did this very night. Do you think that villain, Pu, will allow me to keep them? Besides," Prince Tung's voice became confiding, "I had no idea that these objects had such a great value. That wretch, my steward, tried to sell them a year ago, and he had the effrontery to tell me that they would fetch almost nothing. Besides, it is only correct that I should make a generous gesture. Tell the young virgin, please, that I cannot disappoint her and tell her to place the funds safely in a Shanghai banking institution which is run by English."

"I am afraid I do not understand," I said. "I thought that you valued your pictures."

Prince Tung waved his delicate hand in a polite but hopeless gesture.

"There is so much, my valued friend, that you do not understand," he said, "that I am discouraged by your ignorance. I do value my pictures to the extent of the price that is offered."

It was up to me to explain to Eleanor Joyce Prince Tung's mingled sentiments, but I did not know how to explain them lucidly. Instead of framing some adequate explanation, my mind had turned away from Prince Tung and his difficulties about his pictures; the voluble, mercurial chatter of Prince Tung had

271

done something to me that was only half explicable. I know now that it was only the last of a succession of experiences which had been combining over a period of time to change me. Eleanor Joyce, my servant Yao, Prince Tung and Mr. Moto all were in it. They had all conspired to shatter my confidence in my well being. The result made me lonely. It confirmed my reluctant conviction that things would never be quite as they had been before. I had felt that I was a part of the city of Peking; now I knew that this conviction had been illusion, and that I would never be a part of it. I could see myself as others may have seen me, certainly as Eleanor Joyce had seen me — a stranger in a strange country, living in a fool's Paradise; and I could see myself as something uglier than that. I could see myself as one of those misfits who cumber the earth, like spoiled children, incapable of adjustment to the life where they were placed and indulging instead in illusory futilities of existence which certainly were no part of life. I could see myself as one of those unfortunates, unable to face incontrovertible fact, constantly escaping from reality, and at the same time endeavoring to gain applause. That vision of myself made me lonely, empty. More than that, it filled me with distaste.

I do not say that this train of ideas came to my mind just then in any sort of logical sequence. The thing which I experienced was more of an emotion than an idea and the emotion had a personification. It was personified by Eleanor Joyce. I wondered why I had not realized before that she was something which I had always wanted. She stood for something which my own inadequacy had told me I would never have. And now, something had made her worth everything else. She had been strong enough to be herself without any affectation. She had conceded nothing. I had entirely forgotten Prince Tung and his pictures.

"Eleanor," I said, and stopped, amazed at and distrustful of the impulse that was making me speak.

"What is it, Tom?" she asked.

I looked around the room and cleared my throat. I looked at Prince Tung who was pouring himself a cup of tea. I looked at the blue and red and green patterns on the rafters and at my red lacquer desk and at the paper windows, and then I looked at Eleanor Joyce. She was not the sort that ever would go native.

"What is it, Tom?" she said again, "aren't you feeling well?"

I was not. I doubt if one ever is when one is struggling with emotion.

"Eleanor," I said, "do you think that I amount to anything?"

273

"Don't be stupid," she answered. "Of course I think you do." I was humbly grateful to her for her opinion and I wanted to tell her so, but instead I said:

"Eleanor, let's get out of here."

"Out where? What do you mean?" she asked. It would have taken me a long while to have explained to her exactly what I meant. I waved my hand in a helpless circle that embraced the objects in the room.

"You have rather broken this thing up for me," I said. "Don't ask me how, because I couldn't answer you. I don't even know what I mean exactly, but you've broken this thing up. If I stayed here, I'd keep thinking of you. Last night I had a letter. They want me to come back. They want me back at home."

"Well, why don't you go?" she said. Her expression was curious. I believe she knew perfectly well what I was trying to say.

"I can't go. I won't, unless you go too," I answered.

She was smiling at me. "Is this serious?" she asked.

"Yes," I said. "Damned serious."

Her smile grew broader. "That's the clumsiest proposal I've ever had," she said. "And not so dreadfully complimentary, either."

"Well," I said, "it doesn't matter, does it?"

"No," she said. "I don't suppose it does. I shall be delighted to get out of here. Thank you for suggesting it."

Then Prince Tung was speaking. He had set down

274

his cup of tea and his voice chimed inopportunely into our discussion.

"I trust you have explained about the pictures," he said. "And that everything is satisfactory."

"It is not so," I told him. "My mind wandered. I was not speaking about the pictures. I have asked Miss Joyce to marry me."

Prince Tung raised a delicate hand and dropped it back on his knee.

"But I do not understand," he said. "This is inconsequential. Surely this is not a way even your peculiar people embark on such a problem. Why do you wish to marry her?"

"Because I love her," I said.

"That is one thing," said Prince Tung. "Personally I have loved many women. Marriage is another."

It occurred to me that I had forgotten something.

"Excuse me," I said to Prince Tung. "There is something I must tell the lady." And I spoke to Eleanor Joyce.

"Eleanor," I said. "I love you."

"I know you do," she answered. "It's lucky for you I know it." Then I was kissing her, without having known that I was going to. And I heard Prince Tung saying:

"This is amazing. I do not understand."

And I did not understand whether circumstances had altered me or whether I had altered circum-

275

stances. There was no opportunity just then to apologize or to explain my actions to Prince Tung, because my servant Yao appeared in the courtyard doorway in a clean, white, cotton gown.

"The Japanese, Mr. Moto, is approaching," he said, "and refreshment will be ready in a few minutes. I trust the master is comfortable. I trust the master is pleased with his servant."

"Don't disturb yourself," I told him. "Words cannot express my pleasure." I did not care to express exactly what I felt about him. I actually felt kindly toward him, although I knew he was a rascal. I felt kindly toward the Orient and toward the Western world.

Mr. Moto appeared, exactly as he had promised. Although he must have been very busy since I had seen him last, he had found time to wash and change. He was dressed in a fresh black and white checked suit. Its pattern was blatantly large, selected, I imagine, from some idea that it represented the height of European fashion. Mr. Moto's smile was broader than I have ever seen it. It was evident that he was very, very pleased.

"Everything is nice," said Mr. Moto. "Very, very nice." He rubbed his hands together as though he were warming them before the fire. "There will be no incident to-night. Everything is very, very calm.

Have you some whiskey, my dear chap? Good whiskey for good friends, what? Here is looking at you, what? Yes. Everything is very, very nice. No, there will be no disturbance. The police here are not bad. The City will be under martial law to-morrow morning but you shall have a pass, of course. And Miss Joyce, of course. But if it is convenient, I think Miss Joyce should stay here for a little while, although I am afraid it may not be quite proper."

"Thank you," said Miss Joyce. "As long as Mr. Nelson is sure he wants me."

Mr. Moto bowed and took a long sip from his whiskey glass.

"I am very grateful to you," he said. "You have not helped only me to-night, but what is more important, you have helped my country. It would have been serious just now if anything should have happened. It would have interfered with other plans which are more practical. I cannot explain. Please do not ask me to explain."

I knew better than to ask him. But there was one thing that worried me.

"But what has happened to Wu Lo Feng and Mr. Takahara?" I asked him. "Did you catch them before they got loose? They must have got away."

Mr. Moto's smile grew broader. I was reminded again that the smile of a Japanese does not necessarily denote humor. It may be used equally well to cover up embarrassment and pain. Mr. Moto's smile was purely mechanical, purely a piece of politeness.

"Oh," he said. "I am very, very sorry but they will make no more trouble. You see — " Mr. Moto rubbed his hands together, "that is why I was delayed when we were leaving that room to-night. I was so sorry I could not come directly when you called — so very sorry."

"How do you mean?" I asked him. I was sorry myself the moment I asked because I should have known the answer.

Mr. Moto's eyes were on me, narrow and inscrutable. "Of course," he said, "Mr. Takahara could not live. Although I was very, very sorry. It was different with Wu Lo Feng. He might have been very, very useful to me under certain circumstances. But then I considered that he might be difficult for you. So I was obliged to liquidate them. Do not thank me. I am so very grateful. I am so very glad. He was not a very nice man. But shall we talk of something pleasant?"

Eleanor Joyce walked toward him and held out her hand.

"Yes," she said, "let's. Thank you, Mr. Moto."

THE END